Imprisoned
—in the—
Golden City

Trailblazer Books

*Hero Tales: A Family Treasury of True Stories
From the Lives of Christian Heroes* (Volumes I, II, III, & IV)

*Curriculum guide available.
Written by Julia Pferdehirt with Dave & Neta Jackson.   02C

Imprisoned
–in the–
Golden City

Dave & Neta Jackson

Story illustrations by
Julian Jackson

BETHANY HOUSE PUBLISHERS
MINNEAPOLIS, MINNESOTA 55438

Published by Bethany House Publishers
A Ministry of Bethany Fellowship International
11400 Hampshire Avenue South
Minneapolis, Minnesota 55438
www.bethanyhouse.com

Printed in the United States of America by
Bethany Press International, Minneapolis, Minnesota 55438

Library of Congress Cataloging-in-Publication Data

Jackson, Dave.
    Imprisoned in the Golden City / Dave & Neta Jackson.
        p.   cm. — (Trailblazer Books)
    Summary: As the Burmese War begins in the 1820s, missionaries Adoniram and Ann Judson, the adoptive parents of May-lo and Len-lay, are accused of espionage.
        1. Judson, Adoniram, 1788–1850—Juvenile fiction.
    2. Judson, Ann Hasseltine, 1789–1826—Juvenile fiction.
    [1. Judson, Adoniram, 1788–1850—Fiction. 2. Judson, Ann Hasseltine, 1789–1826—Fiction. 3. Missionaries—Fiction.
    4. Burmese War, 1824–1826—Fiction. 5. Burma—History—Fiction. 6. Christian life—Fiction.]
    I. Jackson, Neta. II. Title. III. Series.
PZ7.J132418Im   1993
[Fic]—dc20   92–46181
ISBN 1–55661–269–9   CIP
                                                                 AC

All the characters and the basic events following American missionaries Adoniram and Ann Judson during the prison years in Burma from 1823-1826 are true. The Judsons did take in two foster Burmese girls, and Mr. Rodgers did have a half-Burmese son. The children's Burmese names, however, were not known.

The timing of the events at Oung-Pen-La has been adjusted slightly to help simplify the story, and the tiger in the cage was actually a lioness. Also, it is not known whether Dr. Price's blind wife came to live at the mission house while her husband was in prison, and it was probably Maung Ing who found the prison pillow and rescued its contents.

CONTENTS

DAVE AND NETA JACKSON are a full-time husband/wife writing team who have authored and coauthored many books on marriage and family, the church, relationships, and other subjects. Their books for children include the TRAILBLAZER series and *Hero Tales* Volumes I, II, and III. The Jacksons have two married children, Julian and Rachel, and make their home in Evanston, Illinois.

Chapter 1

Wild Woman

SQUATTING ON THE OPEN PORCH of the little bamboo house on the outskirts of the city of Rangoon, Len-Lay didn't see the shadowy figure crouching in the dark below. The house, like many in the country of Burma in 1823, stood off the ground on four-foot-high stilts. Pigs grunted contentedly underneath; scrawny chickens had ceased their endless pecking as night fell and were roosting among the stilts.

The dark-haired girl hummed softly as she stirred vegetables into a bubbling pot of chicken stew. She felt very grown-up as she checked the hot coals in the container beneath the pot; the embers were glowing brightly. The twelve-year-old rocked back on her heels smugly. Ever since her mother had gone away the previous year, Len-Lay had been doing all the cooking and cleaning—with Mah-Lo's help, of course.

Len-Lay wondered about her younger sister . . . Mah-Lo should have been back with the waterpot by now. If she didn't come back soon, the broth would boil away and the stew would burn. Len-Lay squinted impatiently into the smoky dusk of the December evening.

Then she spotted her. A small figure tottered unsteadily between the crowded row of stilt-houses, balancing a waterpot on her shoulder. Len-Lay hopped to her feet, snatched up a bowl of steamed rice, and hurried inside. "*Aphe!* Father!" she called, setting the rice on the eating mat spread in the center of the room. "Mah-Lo's coming. We can eat—"

The sound of a terrified scream tore through the quiet house.

Maung Shway-Bay, writing a letter by candlelight in a corner of the room, leaped to his feet and knocked over the stool that held his inkpot. "Mah-Lo!" he cried, rushing past his oldest daughter and out onto the porch. Len-Lay, her heart pounding, cautiously followed and peered around her father's broad back.

Ten-year-old Mah-Lo was writhing in the grip of a wild-looking creature and screaming at the top of her lungs. The waterpot had fallen and its contents spilled. The woman—was it a woman?—clasped the girl with long, bony arms; her hair stood out in all directions, framing large, fierce eyes. Worst of all, the wild woman was laughing, a high-pitched cackle that made little bumps rise on Len-Lay's skin.

Maung Shway-Bay gripped the bamboo porch railing in shocked silence. Why was her father frozen in place? Why didn't he do something?

Then Len-Lay heard him gasp. "Mah Kyi!"

Her mother? Could it possibly be—

"Yesss! Mah Kyi has come back!" the woman hissed as if answering Len-Lay's thoughts.

Mah-Lo stopped screaming, twisted in the woman's grasp, and stared into the wild eyes just inches from her face.

"Let the child go, Mah Kyi," ordered Maung Shway-Bay, starting down from the porch.

"*Stand back!*" the woman screeched. Her husband stopped. That's when Len-Lay realized that neighbors had gathered in the road when they heard the screaming. Maung Shway-Bay held up his hand, signaling them to stay back.

He took a deep breath. "What do you want, Mah Kyi? Why have you come back?"

"Why? *Why?*" Her eyes grew larger and more fierce. "For my children, of course. I am their mother. I have come to take them with me!"

Len-Lay gasped and ran to her father's side.

Maung Shway-Bay's voice trembled a little. "You are sick, Mah Kyi. You cannot take the children. You must go away and rest."

"Sick?" Mah Kyi challenged. "Look how strong I am!" She tightened her arms and lifted Mah-Lo off the ground. The frightened child started to wail loudly and struggle again.

"Let the child go, Mah Kyi! You are frightening her. A mother does not frighten her own children."

Mah Kyi lowered Mah-Lo to the ground. The girl sobbed in the woman's strong grip.

"You are the sick one!" The woman pointed a shaking finger at her husband. "You associate with foreign spies! You listen to their strange God-talk. You have disturbed the *karma* of this house! I will take the girls away, before they go crazy, too!"

Len-Lay's thoughts were swirling. What was her mother talking about? What spies? Did she mean Mr. Judson, the white man who lived in the mission house? Her father did spend a lot of time there studying and talking, and a few years before he had done a strange thing: He let the white man put him under the water of the Irrawaddy River. The missionary called it being baptized, and her father said it meant that now he was a Jesus follower. But . . . that was supposed to be a secret. *All Burmese people must worship Buddha.* It was the law.

"Len-Lay." Her father leaned close to her ear. "Run to your mother's brother. Tell him Mah Kyi has returned. He must come quickly and get her before she harms Mah-Lo—or herself."

Len-Lay gulped. Her uncle's house was three miles outside Rangoon, in a little village to the west. But she obediently scurried down the porch steps.

"Catch her! Catch her!" screeched her mother. "Don't let her get away!"

But the little crowd that stood uncertainly in front of Maung Shway-Bay's house parted and let her slip into the night.

It was morning before Len-Lay finally returned home.

All the way to her uncle's village, she had tried not to think of the tigers that sometimes came out of the forests at night. But the tiny hairs on her neck stood up whenever unseen monkeys shrieked from the tops of the tamarind trees. On and on she hurried until finally the thatched, bamboo houses of her uncle's village took shape in the darkness.

Her mother's brother had listened with a frown as Len-Lay gasped out her story, then without a word headed back down the road toward Rangoon. "Stay here for the night, child," her aunt soothed. "You can return in the morning when it is safe."

Now Len-Lay walked uncertainly into the little fenced-in yard and up the porch steps of her house. She noticed the pot of chicken stew was still on the little stove. All the broth had boiled away and the chicken and vegetables were stuck, hard and cold, on the bottom.

Then she heard her uncle's voice, harsh and accusing.

"Yes, my unfortunate sister is crazy in the head; we will take her away again. But she is right about one thing, Maung Shway-Bay, you associate with false people! You keep a false religion, and you speak false words. What is worse for your children—a crazy mother, or a father who denies his own religion?"

At that moment Maung Shway-Bay saw Len-Lay in the doorway and motioned for her to come in. She soundlessly crossed the bamboo floor and sat next to Mah-Lo, who was half-hidden behind her father.

With a quick glance around the room, Len-Lay saw her mother crumpled passively in the corner, asleep. Her father sat on a stool facing his brother-in-law, hands on his knees.

Len-Lay's uncle sucked in a deep breath. "Rumors are going around the city that the English are preparing to attack Rangoon from the sea. People are also saying that the white people, the so-called missionaries, are really spies who give away our military secrets."

Maung Shway-Bay laughed aloud. "Ridiculous!" he snorted. "They are teachers of Christianity—"

"The religion of the *English*."

"Maybe so. But the missionaries are from America, not England."

Len-Lay's uncle shook his head as he considered this fact. "Nevertheless," he spat out, "only evil can come from your association with them. As your brother-in-law, I would be within my rights to beat you, to pound out this evil from our family. Consider what I say!"

The uncle then rose abruptly, went over to the corner and shook the woman awake. "Come, sister. We must go."

Mah Kyi opened her eyes and looked around in confusion, as if she didn't know where she was. She looked at Len-Lay and Mah-Lo showing no sign of recognition, then meekly allowed her brother to lead her out of the house.

Len-Lay stood with her father and Mah-Lo in the doorway and watched them go. Suddenly Len-Lay buried her face against her father's side. The words of the two men frightened her. Was her father in danger? Would her uncle really beat him?

Len-Lay sank to the floor of the porch and hugged her knees. She was shaking all over. Everything was wrong! When her mother first started acting strange and had to go away, Len-Lay had cried herself to sleep every night. Gradually, she had gotten used to her mother's absence . . . and now she had shown up again, so different, so . . . so terrible.

Len-Lay felt as if she were being torn in two. She wanted her mother back—the pretty, laughing mother who had combed Len-Lay's long, dark hair as a little girl and taught her how to coil it on top of her head. Len-Lay had loved to wear pretty combs and flowers in her hair in an effort to look like her mother.

But *this* woman—this wild, cackling woman—how could she be her mother? Len-Lay shuddered. She had been so frightened watching Mah-Lo struggle in Mah Kyi's fierce grip. She was relieved she was gone!

Len-Lay beat her small fists against her knees. *Gone! Gone! Gone!* Then hot tears poured down her cheeks. "Oh, mother . . . my poor mother," she moaned.

After a long time, Len-Lay felt her father's hand on her shoulder. "Eldest daughter, you must dry your tears and help your sister pack. It is no longer safe here. We must go to the mission house."

The two Burmese girls stood on either side of their father in the mission yard, each holding a bundle of clothing. Len-Lay wore a blue silk *longyi*— a long skirt wound about her body—with a short white tunic. Gold bracelets, necklaces, and anklets made her nut-brown skin glow.

Mah-Lo was similarly dressed in a lemon yellow *longyi*. They nervously gripped their father's *patso*, the loose flowing trousers he created by knotting a piece of bright-colored silk around his waist and legs.

The girls stared at the strange man and woman who came to meet them. Though they had both been to the mission house before, they had never gotten used to the pale skin of Adoniram and Ann Judson.

He wore a funny black jacket and black trousers; she wore a white blouse with long sleeves and lace at her throat; her heavy skirt was a dull brown.

Mah-Lo giggled and Len-Lay knew what she was thinking. *Didn't these foreigners like pretty colors?*

"Quiet!" their father hissed. Then Maung Shway-Bay spoke to the missionaries.

"Teacher, I come to ask a favor. My unfortunate wife is sick in her mind, and I had to send her away. Also, my brother-in-law—and even my own brother— has threatened to beat me because I now follow Jesus. I beg you, take my girls into your house. Teach them to read so they can read Jesus' words on the paper you have written."

Adoniram Judson's smile turned to deep concern and he looked at his wife. Then he pointed toward a pile of crates and boxes that stood in the mission yard. "Dear brother, we are leaving Rangoon," he said in Burmese. "We sail tomorrow for Ava, the Golden City, to build a second mission house there. I have only been waiting for Mrs. Judson to return from America. Surely, you don't want us to take your children so far—"

Len-Lay shivered with fear and excitement. Leave Rangoon? *No, no!* She did not want to go so far away from her father. But *Ava*, home of the emperor, lord of all air and water . . . she never dreamed she might travel so far!

For a moment Maung Shway-Bay looked confused. Then his face became resolute once more. "Yes. I will let them go. Take my motherless daughters into your home under your protection. Teach them to read."

For a moment no one spoke. Nervously Len-lay looked around. She noticed a strange chair sitting among the packing boxes. It had two curved pieces of wood stuck to the bottom of the legs. She thought that if someone sat in it, it would surely tip right over!

Then she heard Mrs. Judson say, "Adoniram, if Maung Shway-Bay's girls went with us, I could begin my school for girls in Ava right away."

"But, Ann!" her husband protested. "You have just returned from a long voyage; you have only recently recovered your health after a long illness. Are you sure you are up to mothering two half-grown children?"

Mrs. Judson's eyes shone with unshed tears, but her voice never wavered. "God saw fit to take our baby, Roger. My arms have been empty. Now it seems God will fill them with these dear girls."

Mr. Judson tenderly brushed a strand of hair from his wife's face. "Well, then," he said, turning back to Maung Shway-Bay, "it is settled."

Chapter 2

War Canoes and River Bandits

THE GIRLS DID NOT CLING to their father when he left, but merely *sheekoed* (bowed) politely. But Len-Lay felt a lump in her throat as she watched him walk swiftly down the road. She put a protective arm around her sister.

After Maung Shway-Bay was out of sight, Mrs. Judson knelt down and gave Len-Lay and Mah-Lo each a warm hug. "You remind me of my younger sisters back in America when I was growing up," she said, as they climbed the little steps to the mission house. Len-Lay saw that it was just like their own bamboo house on stilts, only larger. "I will call you Mary Hasseltine," she said smiling at Len-Lay; and to Mah-Lo, "and I will call you Abby Hasseltine, after my two sisters."

Len-Lay didn't know what to think. Everything was happening so fast!

The mission house was very crowded. Two other missionary couples from America would stay behind to support the little Rangoon church with its eighteen baptized believers. One of the couples had just arrived with Mrs. Judson from America and did not speak any Burmese. So all day long there was a babble of English as the new missionaries unpacked and the Judsons packed.

On her way home from America, Mrs. Judson had also hired a Bengali cook named Koo-Chill who already seemed devoted to her. "Mrs. *Yoodthan* hired me," he said,  pronouncing "Judson" the Burmese way. "If she goes to Ava, I also go!"

In all the excitement of the last twenty-four hours, Len-Lay and Mah-Lo didn't realize how hungry they were until they smelled the curried rice and vegetables Koo-Chill had cooked for supper. They ate heartily, and Len-Lay secretly thought it was nice to eat someone else's cooking for a change.

After supper, Adoniram and Ann Judson walked arm and arm to the little grove of mango trees behind the mission house. The girls, who had not left Ann's side all afternoon, hesitated. But she smiled and beckoned them to come along and enjoy the cool of the winter evening.

The Judsons stopped beside a little grave. "This is where we buried our baby Roger," Mrs. Judson told the girls quietly. "If he had lived, he would be eight years old. But . . . he went to be with Jesus before his first birthday."

Len-Lay looked at Mah-Lo, wondering what she meant, "went to be with Jesus"? Wasn't the baby dead?

Mrs. Judson went on, speaking softly, remembering: "Our first baby was born dead while we were still on the ship coming to Burma. We miss them both, terribly. But someday we will see them again, when we go to live with Jesus forever."

Later that night, the girls lay on the soft pallets Mrs. Judson had made up for them. "The foreign missionaries say strange things," Len-Lay whispered to Mah-Lo. "No one lives forever—not even Buddha himself! The priests say we might be reborn several times as a different person, depending on how good we are in this life. But the final state of perfection is nothingness."

A deep breath was her only answer. Mah-Lo was fast asleep, and Len-Lay was left alone with her thoughts. She did not understand the Christian message, but the idea of final "nothingness" felt as dreadful in her heart as leaving her father.

❖ ❖ ❖ ❖

Only when the girls carried their bundles aboard the boat Mr. Judson had hired to take them 350 miles up the Irrawaddy River did Len-Lay feel a rush of panic.

"W—will we ever see Father again?" whispered Mah-Lo, her chin quivering. Len-Lay couldn't answer; the lump in her throat was too big. They huddled together on a big coil of rope and watched as Koo-Chill immediately started a fire in his little portable stove right behind the bamboo cabin. Mr. Judson and a fisherman named Maung Ing were loading bundles of household goods onto the deck.

"Maung Ing is coming, too," Mrs. Judson said, sitting down beside the girls. "He was one of the first Burmans to be baptized. But his wife just divorced him for becoming a Christian." She studied the girls' sad faces. "It's not easy following Jesus. But we will help one another be strong, dear Mary . . . dear Abby," she said, calling the girls by their new names and giving them a comforting hug.

The fisherman hung a bamboo cage from the corner of the cabin. "Oh, look!" Mrs. Judson laughed. "Maung Ing has brought his pet parrot along! Have you met Mr. Beg Pardon?"

Len-Lay and Mah-Lo smiled in spite of the sorrow in their hearts. The colorful green bird cocked its head and looked at the girls curiously.

As the grownups busied themselves with the loading, Len-Lay and Mah-Lo decided to explore the little boat that would be their home for several weeks. Walking back toward the stern, however, Len-Lay suddenly jumped and gave a shriek.

There, coiled underneath the perch of the steersman, was a gigantic python.

Len-Lay grabbed Mah-Lo and turned to run—and crashed right into Mrs. Judson. Speechless, the girl pointed toward the snake with a trembling finger.

Mrs. Judson tensed. "Parrots, yes; snakes, no!" she said grimly to the captain, who came to see what was the matter.

"The lord snake?" said the wiry captain. "He belongs to the boat! He will keep the robbers away."

"But—but he might harm us!" Len-Lay protested, backing away from the giant python who had turned an eye on them. She hated snakes, even more than tigers. Mah-Lo said nothing, but her eyes were bulging.

The captain grinned, showing several missing teeth. "Never," he said soothingly, "as long as we keep him full of rice. But I tell you, the boat does not sail without lord python."

The captain would not budge, and in the end, Ann Judson yielded. "We will have nerves of steel by the time we get to Ava!" she joked to the girls. Len-Lay was still uneasy, and kept a wary eye on the snake.

Finally the boat was loaded and the other missionaries came on board to say farewell. "I have only one concern," Len-Lay heard one of them say quietly to Mr. Judson. "The emperor keeps threatening war with the English along the Bengali border. His top general, Bandula, is like a pesky puppy nipping at the heels of an English bulldog. British soldiers may follow you up the river seeking to put a stop to General Bandula's annoying army."

Len-Lay frowned. For the first time she remembered what her mother and uncle had said: that the Judsons were spies for the English. Mah-Lo remembered, too, and was looking at her anxiously.

"Don't worry," Len-Lay whispered. "The Judsons have been very kind to us."

"But if the emperor catches us with *spies* . . ." Mah-Lo whispered back. It was well-known that traitors were thrown into the terrible Death Prison or trampled by the emperor's elephants.

Just then the captain shouted, "The tide has turned! Cast off! Cast off!"

The other missionaries hurried to get off the boat and helped push it out into the tide. The crew poled the boat carefully between dozens of fishing boats. Seeing the white foreigners, peddlers paddled out from shore in their little flat-bottomed skiffs, loudly calling out to sell mangoes, bananas, coconuts, baskets, and beautiful cloth.

The thatched huts of Rangoon crowded right up to the banks of the Irrawaddy River where it flowed into the Gulf of Martaban. Beyond Rangoon, the river headed north, and was Burma's main "highway" into the interior. When the outgoing tide had carried the boat beyond the river traffic, the crew put up the sail, and the steersman skillfully caught the wind by tacking back and forth.

Suddenly Len-Lay caught a glimpse of a round, golden spire rising majestically above the lush trees along the riverbank. "Look!" She pointed. "The Shwe Dagon Pagoda!"

Koo-Chill stopped fussing with his stove and gazed in awe at the massive temple, which contained eight hairs from the head of Gautama Buddha, the founder of Buddhism who lived in the sixth century B.C., and whose name means "the enlightened one."

The Bengali cook had never seen Burma's holiest shrine, and his short week in Rangoon after arriving with Mrs. Judson did not include being a tourist.

"Shwe Dagon is almost a city in itself," Len-Lay said to the plump cook, her pride in Rangoon's famous pagoda overcoming her shyness. "The stonework is so fine that it looks like lace."

"And the only time the priests leave the pagoda is to go begging with their begging bowls," Mah-Lo piped up.

"Shwe Dagon Pagoda is indeed a great monument," said Mr. Judson, joining the children and Koo-Chill as they watched the shimmering gold spire finally slip into the distance. "But God is not in a golden temple. He is in heaven, and His Holy Book tells us how His Spirit can come and live in our hearts."

Koo-Chill shrugged good-naturedly. "I am your cook, honored teacher, not your disciple. I follow you to Ava, but I follow Buddha in my head."

Mr. Judson laughed. "We are glad to have you along, Koo-Chill. But we will talk again, yes?"

Day after day the crowded boat sailed slowly up the Irrawaddy River. Gradually Len-Lay and Mah-Lo began to get used to their new names, as everyone followed Mrs. Judson's example and called them "Mary" and "Abby."

In spite of being surrounded by the two girls, a

cook, a Burmese disciple, and several crewmen, Adoniram and Ann Judson acted like a couple on their honeymoon. They spent long hours holding hands—Ann sitting in the funny chair that rocked back and forth, Adoniram perched on the baggage— as Ann told all about her long journey back to America. The sea voyage and lengthy rest with her family had helped her recover from the illness that had tormented her so long in Rangoon.

Len-Lay could hardly believe her new foster mother had ever been sick. The white woman's cheeks were rosy and her eyes sparkled with good health. Mr. Judson's eyes seemed captivated by his lovely wife. "My dear Ann," he murmured often. It had been a long, lonely two-year separation.

"But I finally got the New Testament translated into the Burmese language," Mr. Judson told his wife gratefully. "And the mission board sent us a doctor while you were gone. But the emperor heard about his skill with a knife and ordered him to come to Ava." He chuckled. "Dr. Price was quite a hit in the king's court—he seems to be good at cutting off infected cysts and eye cataracts. But . . ." His voice trailed off.

Mrs. Judson was combing Mah-Lo's long, dark hair. It had become a daily ritual: the girls sat on deck (out of sight of "lord python!") while Mrs. Judson combed their hair and coiled it on top of their heads in the Burmese fashion.

"But what?" she prompted her husband.

Mr. Judson shook his head. "The royal court fascinates Dr. Price; now he thinks he's the king's best friend! I worry about him. He doesn't realize how fickle Burmese royalty can be."

He brightened, "At least King Bagyidaw is now willing to let us set up a mission house in Ava. That is, he was when I left the good doctor performing his surgical miracles!"

Their conversation was interrupted when the boat was tied up near a river village, so that Koo-Chill could buy food and supplies from the local marketplace. Everyone went ashore to stretch their legs, but they drew a noisy crowd of villagers who had never seen a white woman before.

Len-Lay felt strange walking hand in hand with her foster mother. She liked both Mr. and Mrs. Judson; they were kind to the girls and tried to make them feel at home. But people in the villages looked at the girls warily, as if . . . as if the foreigners had bewitched the girls or something.

The tears came at night as the girls lay on their pallets in the little boat cabin. Each day took them farther from Rangoon. When would they see their father again? They tried not to make any noise, but Ann Judson sensed their distress. She sometimes sat by their pallets in the darkness, stroking their hair and humming a song.

Daytime was easier. As the boat sailed steadily mile after mile up the wide river, the sisters stared at the abandoned cities that stood in ruins along the riverbank. Creeping vines covered gigantic white stone pagodas and once-magnificent palaces. Monkeys, from their perch on crumbling statues of Buddha, scolded the travelers.

"Each new emperor wanted his own royal city," Maung Ing explained to the girls and Koo-Chill. "The old cities were left to rot in the jungle. We'll see more of them before this trip is over." Mr. Beg Pardon, sitting on Maung Ing's shoulder, bobbed his head as if to agree.

"Be quiet! Be alert!" snapped the captain as they approached the deserted city of Pagan. It was here that Buddhism had been declared the state religion of Burma eight centuries before. The boat and its passengers glided silently past the ghostly ruins. The crew stood alert with muskets ready, watching the riverbanks.

"Sometimes the *dacoits*, river bandits, hide out in the ruins and attack passing boats," the captain later explained to his passengers. "We have been fortunate. You see, the lord python has kept the robbers away!" And he smiled his toothless grin.

Just then Len-Lay heard Mr. Judson mutter as he pointed upriver, "Then what do you call this?"

The boat had just sailed around a bend in the river, and there, coming toward them along the far side, was a fleet of huge, golden canoes. Each looked as if it had been made from a single, immense teak tree, six to eight feet wide. The sterns rose high where the steersmen stood; each boat was teeming with soldiers armed with spears and muskets. Bright flags and banners flew by the hundreds, and paddlers were driven on by the steady beat of drums.

And in the middle of the fleet was a magnificent golden barge.

Mah-Lo began jumping up and down. *"Dacoits! Dacoits!"* The younger girl's eyes were wide and her teeth chattered.

"Awwwk! Dacoits!" squawked Mr. Beg Pardon.

"No! Not *dacoits*! It is the Golden Fist," gasped the captain, "the emperor's war boats. And the barge . . . it is General Bandula himself!"

Then one of the war canoes detached itself from the fleet and with strong, swift strokes raced across the river toward the little boat. Ann Judson pulled Len-Lay and Mah-Lo close to her.

A soldier stood in the bow of the golden canoe, waving a long spear. "Stop in the name of the emperor!" he yelled.

The crew of the little boat quickly lowered the sail.

As the war canoe came alongside, several soldiers, including the man with the spear, jumped on board. "Capture him!" the soldier yelled, pointing the spear at Mr. Judson's chest. "The English spy is our prisoner!"

Chapter 3

Ice on the Golden Feet

A T THE SOLDIER'S ACCUSATION, the boat captain and crew immediately fell to their faces on the deck.

"I am innocent! I am innocent!" moaned the captain. "I had no idea—"

Mr. Judson gave the captain's prostrate body a nudge with his toe. "If you will quit blubbering, I will straighten this out," he said sternly.

Ann Judson's arms tightened around the girls as the soldiers stepped forward threateningly. Len-Lay's mouth went dry; were they all going to be prisoners?

Mr. Judson held up his hand. "I am an *American*," he said firmly. "My wife and I are on our way to the Golden City at the command of King Bagyidaw himself."

The soldier with the spear hesitated.

"We are under orders to capture all English spies!" he repeated gruffly.

"Of course," Mr. Judson agreed pleasantly. "But we are not English. The emperor will be angry if you hinder our journey. We, too, are under orders—to return to the Golden Throne with all possible speed."

The soldier slowly lowered his spear, then abruptly turned on the captain. "Get up! Be on your way!" he barked. "Why is your sail down? Up! Up!"

"Up! Up!" mimicked Mr. Beg Pardon from his wicker cage.

The crew scrambled to put up the sail as the soldiers bounded into their great golden canoe and sent it skimming back to the fleet. Everyone else stared wide-eyed at the retreating soldiers.

Then Koo-Chill began to laugh, his big chest bouncing with each guffaw. As the tension dissolved, Maung Ing, the Judsons, and the girls joined in. Only the captain still scowled, his dignity ruffled.

"It may be 'lord snake' who keeps the robbers away," Koo-Chill wheezed, "but it is Mr. *Yoodthan* who turns back the whole Burmese army!"

Six weeks after leaving Rangoon, the little boat and its tired passengers and crew sighted Ava, the Golden City, home of the emperor. They glimpsed great pagodas and palaces through the palm trees; rough bamboo shacks crowded the riverbanks. It was January 23, 1824.

As the boat threaded its way through the usual mob of fishing boats and peddlers' skiffs, they heard someone shouting, "Hello! Adoniram! Over here!"

"Hello! Hello!" squawked Mr. Beg Pardon.

A man in a small boat was approaching from the opposite bank, waving and calling. Mr. Judson smiled and waved back. "It's Jonathan Price come to meet us."

A tall, gawky foreigner soon scrambled aboard. Len-Lay and Mah-Lo stared. This strange American was even taller than Mr. Judson, but thinner, and he seemed to be all arms and legs. His straw-colored hair bristled as if he'd just had a fright.

"Adoniram!" he said, shaking Mr. Judson's hand eagerly. "And this must be your dear wife." Dr. Price grabbed Ann Judson's slender hand and pumped it vigorously. "Welcome! Welcome!"

As he turned back to Mr. Judson, the doctor's smile faded and his forehead puckered in an anxious frown. "You must come and stay at my house across the river. I have urgent things to tell you. Come, come. Follow me."

Dr. Price was back in his little boat and paddling

toward the opposite bank before the Judsons could introduce the rest of their party. But several hours later the Judsons, Maung Ing, and the girls were sharing a meal with Dr. Price in the brick house he had recently built overlooking the river. Koo-Chill, however, refused to budge from his own "kitchen" aboard the boat.

The house was very damp and Len-Lay shivered. The new bricks did not seem fully dry. Medical instruments, books, and papers were scattered everywhere. "Neatness isn't one of Jonathan's virtues," she heard Mr. Judson whisper to Ann. "His wife died shortly after he arrived in Burma. He's definitely not suited to bachelorhood."

A Burmese woman served the meal. She squinted constantly and brought everything up close to her face to see it.

"Her name is Ma-Noo, my housekeeper," Dr. Price explained. "She has an eye disease—cataracts. I hope to operate on her one of these days soon." His frown deepened. "But recently I have been so distracted, I cannot take care of my patients. I don't understand it! Overnight, everything has changed!"

"What are you talking about, Jonathan?" asked Mr. Judson.

"The king! He refuses to see me. Me! His own friend and doctor." Dr. Price shook his head sadly. "Talk of war is everywhere, and suddenly all foreigners are mistrusted. I have tried and tried to tell King Bagyidaw that I am an American, not English; that I am his loyal subject. But he acts as if I am not there!"

35

Dr. Price lapsed into a dejected silence. Then, almost as an afterthought, he burst out, "I don't know what this means for setting up a second mission in Ava. You must go to the palace, Adoniram, and try to talk to the king."

"The king has already given us a little plot of land along the river to build a *kyoung*," Mr. Judson reminded him. A kyoung was a house for religious teachers to live in.

"But will he let you preach? Don't take Maung Ing with you to the palace. I don't think the king is in the mood to meet a Burman who has received Christian baptism." Dr. Price made an effort to cheer up. "Well, until you build the *kyoung*, you can all stay here—"

They had finished their meal of rice and vegetables and tea. Mrs. Judson leaned toward the girls and said quietly, "Mary and Abby, would you please help Ma-Noo?"

Len-Lay thought Mrs. Judson looked strange. But the girls obediently cleared away the bowls and helped the nearly blind housekeeper scrub and put away the cooking pots while the three Americans talked.

Suddenly the girls heard a thud and Mr. Judson cried out, "Ann!" Running into the room, Len-Lay and Mah-Lo saw that Mrs. Judson had fallen off her chair. Mr. Judson was at her side.

"I—I'm all right, Adoniram," whispered Mrs. Judson, struggling to sit up. "Just a touch of fever; it made me light-headed."

"It's the dampness in the bricks," said Mr. Judson grimly. "Jonathan, we appreciate your invitation. But I think we will have to stay on the boat until we build a mission house."

It took two weeks to build a bamboo house—three rooms and an open porch—on the little plot of land by the river that the king had given Mr. Judson on his last trip to Ava. As soon as it was finished, Mr. Judson hired workers to begin building a more permanent house right beside it. Only a brick house would help keep out the stifling-hot temperatures when summer arrived. But they would make sure the bricks had fully dried before they moved in.

Even before they finished the temporary house, Mr. Judson went to the palace to see the emperor. Mrs. Judson tried to begin reading lessons for Len-Lay and Mah-Lo on the deck of the boat, but all three kept looking up to see whether Mr. Judson was coming.

Finally, they saw his black hat weaving its way through the crowd of Burmese turbans. As he stepped onto the deck of their "house boat," Maung Ing and Mrs. Judson peppered him with questions.

"Did you see King Bagyidaw?"

"Did he talk to you?"

"Does he support the mission?"

"Will he let you preach?"

Mr. Beg Pardon got excited by all the hubbub,

added a few squawks of his own.

Mr. Judson just shook his head and sat down on a coil of rope—*awfully close to 'lord python,'* Len-Lay thought. "He acted as if he didn't know me, just like Dr. Price warned us," he said. "I bowed low before the 'Golden Feet,' but it was as

if they were made of ice! The emperor neither looked at nor spoke to me."

Maung Ing looked troubled. "This is not good, my brother. If the king ignores the foreign teacher in his presence, he will surely not allow you to preach in Ava! And what will he do if he finds out that Maung Ing has left Buddha to follow the Jesus way?" The fisherman looked distressed.

"We must trust God," Mrs. Judson said quickly. "God has brought us—all of us—to Ava for a purpose. We will just have to try again."

Twice more Mr. Judson went to the royal court, trying to speak to the emperor; twice more he got an icy reception. But once the bamboo house on stilts was finished and the Judsons, Len-Lay and Mah-Lo, Koo-Chill, Maung Ing and Mr. Beg Pardon had moved in, Mr. Judson had an idea. "Tomorrow we will go see Mr. Rodgers."

Mr. Rodgers, Adoniram Judson explained, was an Englishman who had become a Burmese citizen many years before. He held an official position in King Bagyidaw's court, as he had for the previous king. "Maybe Rodgers will put in a good word for us."

Mr. Judson smiled at Len-Lay and Mah-Lo. "We'll all go—the whole family. Maybe these charming young ladies will succeed where we old Americans have failed!"

Mr. Rodgers' house was spacious and ornate—a far cry from the little bamboo mission house. A servant invited Mr. and Mrs. Judson and the two girls into a sitting room where they waited for Mr. Rodgers to arrive.

Soon the middle-aged man approached them. He wore a long, quilted Burmese tunic, flowing *patso* trousers and sandals. His gray beard hung, goatlike, in a long tuft from his chin. A scowling Burmese boy accompanied him.

As the man stopped in front of them, the girls noticed his intense *blue* eyes!

"What do you want?" the man growled. He spoke in Burmese, but with a decided English accent.

Mr. Judson bent his head in a respectful bow. "I am happy to see you looking so well, Mr. Rodgers," he began. "My family and I have just arrived in the beautiful city of Ava—"

"Nonsense," growled Mr. Rodgers. "I am not well. Things are rotten in Ava. Let's get down to business." He softened a little as he turned toward Mrs. Judson. "Please sit down. This is my son, Myat," he said, indicating the boy. "Myat, please take the young ladies into the garden."

Mah-Lo gripped Len-Lay's hand as they followed the older boy through the house and out into a beautiful garden bursting with lotus bushes, palms, and mango trees.

"My name is Myat Rodgers," said the boy, still scowling. He was about thirteen, a year older than Len-Lay. "Do you live with the foreign missionaries?"

Len-Lay nodded, trying not to smile. Behind the scowl, she knew the boy was very curious. "Our mother is . . . ill, and our father wants us to learn how to read. Mrs. Judson is starting a school for girls. So we have come to live with them."

"The Judsons live in Burma now, so why do they still wear those funny clothes?" he demanded. Without waiting for an answer he said proudly, "My mother is Burmese. My father *was* English, but he has become a citizen of Burma. He has no use for foreigners who do not adopt Burmese ways—and neither do I."

Mah-Lo skipped away, trying to catch a dappled butterfly. It was Len-Lay's turn to be curious. "Have you ever been in the Golden Presence?"

"The emperor? Of course!" said Myat. "We know the whole royal family—even Prince Meng-myat-bo, the king's brother, and the Princess of Sarawaddy. Except . . ." The scowl returned.

"What is the matter?"

Myat seemed to be struggling with whether to say any more. Finally he blurted, "The stupid English are going to ruin everything!"

"You mean, if there is a war?"

"Yes! King Bagyidaw wants to invade Bengal, but the English got there first. Anyone who is English is suddenly out of favor at court. But it's not fair! My father is a loyal Burmese subject, not like . . . like your American missionaries, the Judsons!" Myat glared at Len-Lay.

"What do you mean?" Len-Lay said defensively. The butterfly had disappeared over the garden wall, and Mah-Lo again grasped her older sister's hand.

"Why did the Judsons come to Ava right now?" Myat challenged. "Maybe they are spies for the En-

41

glish. They may pretend to be American missionaries, but how do they make their money? Have you seen them do any work?'"

"I—I . . ." Len-Lay stuttered. Her father was a cloth-seller; Maung Ing was a fisherman; Koo-Chill was a cook. Mr. Judson was always busy—but what did he actually *do* to earn a living?

Myat smiled triumphantly. "He probably gets paid by the British army for supplying helpful information."

"What is Myat saying, Mary?" Mah-Lo said, sensing the tension between them.

"*Mary*? Is that your name?" Myat questioned. "What is yours?" He pointed at Mah-Lo.

"Mrs. Judson calls me Abby," said Mah-Lo. "She said we remind her of her sisters back in America."

"Foreign names!" sneered Myat. "What are your *real* names?"

"Mah-Lo." Mah-Lo lifted her chin stubbornly.

"Len-Lay," said the older girl, frowning. She didn't like this arrogant, quarrelsome boy. He was only half-Burmese, but he made her feel like *she* was the foreigner, just because she and Mah-Lo lived with the Judsons.

Myat lowered his voice and leaned closer to the girls. "You'd better remember your Burmese names," he said darkly. "Because if Mr. Judson is accused of being a spy, two Burmese girls with English names just might be thrown into prison, too, for aiding the enemy!"

Chapter 4

The Human Horse

MARY AND ABBY!" called Mrs. Judson from the house. "We're ready to go now."

Len-Lay and Mah-Lo came running. Myat Rodgers followed.

"No, I cannot help you," Mr. Rodgers was saying curtly. "As I told you, I, myself, am no longer welcome in the royal court. But even if I were, we don't need foreign missionaries here trying to convert the Burmese people from their way of life. This is my advice, Judson: Leave Burma. Take your family and get out while you can."

"Why don't you leave, Rodgers?" asked Mr. Judson, putting on his black hat.

The Englishman's eyes narrowed. "I have been a Burmese citizen for forty years; my wife and son are

Burmese. This is my home—in spite of the king's rude treatment these last few weeks." Mr. Rodgers' words were tinged with bitterness. Turning abruptly, he walked away, followed by Myat, leaving a servant to show the Judsons out.

The street had filled with people of all ages, shoving and calling to one another. "Mr. Rodgers is not a very pleasant man," Ann Judson said to her husband as they tried to push through the crowd. She had to shout to be heard.

Mr. Judson nodded grimly. "He's a disappointed man—like Dr. Price, but with more reason! After forty years of service in the Burmese government, now he's shunned because he's English. I don't think . . . *what* in the world is going on?"

The noise in the street was growing louder. Len-Lay held tight to Mah-Lo's hand, trying not to lose sight of Mr. Judson's black suit and Mrs. Judson's wide-brimmed hat. They could hear the sound of music coming closer. Suddenly, around a corner, came a team of muscular acrobats, turning flips in the dusty street to the cheers of the crowd.

The Judsons grabbed the girls' hands and pulled them into the doorway of a small pagoda as the acrobats went by. Soon a "band" of musicians playing flutes and drums came marching by, followed by female dancers in brightly-colored silk robes.

Suddenly Len-Lay remembered. The "winter" months with their mild temperatures were fading; the hot summer months were just around the corner. She tugged excitedly on Mrs. Judson's sleeve.

"It's *Tabaung*—the biggest festival of the year!" Len-Lay shouted in her ear. "It always takes place just before the New Year."

Mrs. Judson looked confused for a moment. "The New Year? Oh, of course! I forgot!" she said. "March is the last month of the old year in Burma."

Next came several boxers, dressed only in waistcloths and fiercely boxing the air. A crier marching alongside called out the time of a boxing match later in the day. The boxers were followed by a large group of Buddhist priests in yellow robes, swinging incense burners and chanting.

Len-Lay heard Mr. Judson say, "Ann, this pagan festival is no place for a Christian. Let's—"

Then the crowd hushed expectantly. Cries of "Here they come!" rose from a hundred throats. Huge white elephants lumbered into view, elegantly decorated with garlands of flowers, tassels, and rich tapestry.

"White elephants!" gasped Len-Lay. Only one person in all of Burma had white elephants: the emperor himself. But where was he?

Mah-Lo was hopping up and down, trying to see. Mr. Judson picked her up, his own curiosity getting the best of him.

Behind the elephants, ten trumpeters seemed to be blaring: "Make way! Make way! The king! The king!" And then Len-Lay saw the strangest sight: A spectacular gold-covered carriage came into view, but instead of being pulled by horses, six young men were gripping the shafts and running in front of it.

Five of the carriage-pul- lers were Burmans, wearing the distinctive turbans of minor roy- alty. But right in the front ran a hand-  some Englishman. As the carriage drew closer, the young foreigner glanced up at the Judsons standing in the doorway of the pagoda, caught Len-Lay's eye— and winked!

Len-Lay was so surprised, she almost forgot to look at the emperor riding in the carriage. All around, people were bowing low as the king rode by. Even the Judsons lowered their heads respectfully. Len- Lay only got a quick glance of the boyish king—his head held high—before she, too, bowed low. And then the carriage was gone.

All the way home the girls chattered about the spectacle they'd seen. Nothing they had ever seen in Rangoon compared to this.

"The emperor didn't seem very old," Mah-Lo said.

"He's only about thirty," Mr. Judson affirmed. "The first time I came to Ava, five years ago, he had just been named emperor after the death of his father—and he was playing leap-frog in the palace courtyard!"

"No! You're joking!" Mrs. Judson started to laugh.

"The king is also very small—no taller than Len-Lay here. Did you notice his sloping forehead? It's a family trait—some deformity in the bones. Unfortunately his brother, Prince Meng-myat-bo, is crippled, but the king is only bowlegged."

The lord of white elephants is bowlegged? thought Len-Lay. Somehow her idea of what an emperor should look like was being turned upside down. "What about the foreigner?" she asked curiously. "The one pulling the king's carriage? Is he the king's slave?"

Mr. Judson shrugged. "I thought I'd met every Englishman in Burma—there aren't very many. But I've never seen that young man before!"

That very afternoon, Ann Judson started her school for girls. She sat with Len-Lay and Mah-Lo on the porch of the mission house and helped the two girls draw the letters of the Burmese alphabet. Mr. Beg Pardon patiently cleaned his feathers in the cage swinging overhead from the porch roof.

As Len-Lay dipped a sharpened goose-feather into the inkpot, she suddenly remembered the inkpot her father had spilled the night their mother had returned. The memory of her father was sharp and clear . . . he'd been writing a letter.

A pang of homesickness swept over her.

Len-Lay continued tracing the alphabet. Now she was learning to write, just like her father! If she worked hard, maybe she could write a letter to him soon!

A curious crowd of adults and children stood outside the mission house yard, watching the little school in progress. Mrs. Judson stepped down from the porch, and explained to the onlookers that she was beginning a school and she'd be glad to teach girls to read and write.

Some of the adults scoffed: "Boys learn to read

and write, not girls!" But Mrs. Judson just smiled and told them to think about it.

The paper and inkpots had been put away and the girls were helping Koo-Chill put supper on the low table when they heard a cheerful, "Hello! Anybody home?" from outside the yard.

"Hello! Anybody home!" mimicked Mr. Beg Pardon.

Laughing, Len-Lay and Mah-Lo raced to the open door. It was the Englishman, the emperor's "human horse."

But now he was wearing Burmese riding clothes and tying the reins of a beautiful black horse to the bamboo fence. When he saw the girls in the doorway he said, "Ah, the young ladies!" and, grinning, he winked again. "May I introduce myself properly? My name is Henry Gouger." And he bowed from the waist.

Mrs. Judson appeared and graciously invited the stranger to eat supper with them. Koo-Chill muttered something about "uninvited guests" under his breath, but that ended quickly when the young man began exclaiming over the cook's delicious fish soup.

Henry Gouger had arrived in Ava a year ago with his own merchant ship, he said, hoping to make a fortune trading with the Burmese. He had already traded all his English goods—lace, tea, woven cloth, saddles, china dishes, iron tools, pots and pans—for a tremendous supply of gold, silver, and jewels. He was definitely a wealthy man.

"And I'm only twenty-five!" he laughed. Then he

shrugged. "But the Burmese have a silly law that no gold or jewels can leave the country. So here I sit—a rich man, but I can't take it home to England to enjoy!"

Len-Lay's curiosity got the best of her. "But why were you pulling the emperor's carriage. Did he make you his slave?"

Gouger threw back his head and laughed. "Oh, no, just the opposite. Pulling the emperor's carriage is an honor. It's how he shows his appreciation for all the lengthy discussions we've had about astronomy and map-making. And frankly, I get a kick out of playing horse for the king. Only . . ." The twinkling gray eyes suddenly sobered.

"Only you just got told you're no longer welcome at the royal palace," finished Mr. Judson grimly.

Gouger sighed deeply. "How'd you guess? I was wondering when it would happen. I saw old Rodgers get the cold shoulder and knew it was only a matter of time. Yesterday after the festival, a runner arrived with news that English troops had pushed General Bandula back from the Bengali border. I was immediately banished from the courtyard."

Gouger, Maung Ing, the Judsons, and even Koo-Chill talked late into the evening about the possibility of war between Burma and the English. "The English don't want war!" Gouger exclaimed. "But King Bagyidaw takes their reluctance to fight as a sign of weakness. So he keeps pushing, pushing, pushing . . . and I'm afraid he's going to live to regret it."

Bored with war talk, Len-Lay and Mah-Lo cleared

the table, washed up Koo-Chill's pots, then went out on the porch to play with Mr. Beg Pardon.

Later, as Gouger was leaving, Adoniram Judson said, "We've enjoyed your company, Henry. Please come again, and we would especially like you to join us for worship on Sunday—we've been meeting across the river at the house of Dr. Price."

Gouger grinned and shrugged. "Dr. Price, eh? A bumbling idiot, that man. I'm not much of a church man, myself. But, since you have invited me . . . yes, I will come."

Henry Gouger was a frequent visitor at the mission house. Henry and Adoniram, especially, hit it off. Judson appreciated Gouger's knowledge, and the two men spent hours discussing science, geography, and philosophy. As for Gouger, the Judsons provided him with the family he lacked. Mrs. Judson's feminine grace charmed him, and he teased the girls mercilessly.

And to Maung Ing's delight, Gouger stood on the porch and and even spoke politely to Mr. Beg Pardon.

But Judson and Gouger also had their disagreements. Mr. Judson scolded his young friend for some of his questionable business deals and Gouger often made skeptical remarks about "hypocritical religion." But true to his word, the young Englishman joined them at Dr. Price's house on Sundays. Sometimes eight or ten curious Burmans would also crowd into the house for worship.

During the week, Len-Lay and Mah-Lo settled down to a daily routine of lessons with Mrs. Judson. Once they learned the Burmese alphabet, Mrs. Judson began teaching them to read.

"For ... God ... so ... loved ... the ... world ...." Len-lay sounded out each word on the piece of paper Mrs. Judson had given her. She looked up. "What are these writings?"

"This is part of the Bible, our Holy Scriptures," Mrs. Judson said smiling.

"But it's written in Burmese!" said Len-Lay, astonished.

"That's because Mr. Judson is translating the Bible from English into the Burmese language. Your father read some Christian Scriptures in his own language; that is why he decided to become a Jesus follower."

The words and ideas were very strange, Len-Lay thought. *Why did God sacrifice His own Son—just so people could live forever?* But if her father wanted her to understand them, she would keep working hard to learn to read.

There was now a third girl in the school. The wife of one of the royal court officials had heard about Ann Judson's school that taught girls. One day the woman arrived with her daughter in a *palanquin*—a chair carried by poles on the shoulders of two servants. "Teach her to read," she commanded, then swept grandly away.

Len-Lay and Mah-Lo enjoyed having a friend. Besides reading and writing, Mrs. Judson taught the girls to sew and cook and do housekeeping. As April turned into May, the humid heat sometimes made Ann Judson feel ill, but she continued the school from her bed.

One day during lessons, Mr. Judson asked his wife if he could borrow the girls for an errand. "Mary and Abby," he said seriously, "please take this note to Henry Gouger's house. He will give you some money in return. Be very careful not to lose the money—it is all we have to live on for the next month."

Turning to his wife, Judson said quietly, "I would go myself, but Maung Ing just arrived with a message from Dr. Price—some medical crisis has him very upset. Price is on his way here to talk with me now."

The girls skipped happily toward Henry Gouger's house. They hadn't seen their English friend for several days, and he always made them laugh.

Today was no exception. "Princess Mary! Princess Abby!" Gouger exclaimed, bowing low as if they were royalty. "You honor me by your visit. I think this calls for bringing out . . . the peppermints!"

As the girls savored the English peppermint sticks, Len-Lay gave Gouger the note from Mr. Judson.

"Hmm. Another check to cash. All right." Henry Gouger disappeared into his house and soon returned with a bag of silver ticals. "Tuck this into your skirt," he told Len-Lay, "and go straight home."

As the girls threaded their way through the crowded dirt street, they saw a familiar figure standing at the end of the lane watching them. It was Myat Rodgers. Was he spying on them? He stood right in their path, forcing the girls to stop.

"What were you doing at the English trader's house?" he demanded.

None of your business, Len-Lay thought. But Mah-Lo piped up, "Mr. Gouger gave us some money to give to Mr. Judson." Len-Lay glared at her sister.

Myat gave the girls a curious look. Then he said, "I thought you should know that your American missionaries are not what they appear to be. Now I have proof!" He paused to let that sink in, then leaned toward the girls as if sharing a secret.

"The other American, Dr. Price, works with Mr. Judson, right?"

Len-Lay didn't want to say anything, but finally she said, "Yes."

Myat smiled smugly. "I just heard that the 'doctor' tried to operate on a woman with cataracts—and now she is blind as a bat!"

Len-Lay's mouth dropped opened. Who could it be? Not Ma-Noo, the poor housekeeper! Then Len-Lay held up her head and looked Myat stright in the eye. "I don't believe it," she said.

Myat laughed. "It doesn't matter if you believe it—it's true. Judson's American friend is only *pretending* to be a doctor. Now everyone will know he is a fake."

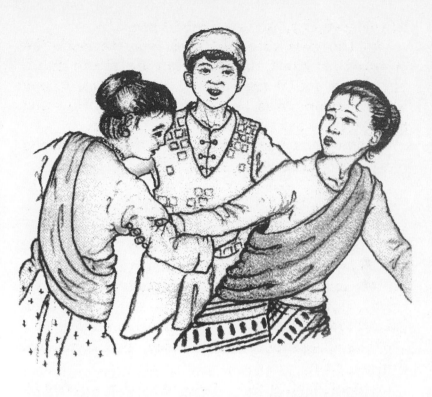

Len-Lay grabbed Mah-Lo's hand, pulled her around Myat, and started running down the street.

"I *told* you the English were paying Mr. Judson!" Myat shouted after them.

Chapter 5

Spotted Faces at the Door

THE GIRLS RAN ALL THE WAY HOME and then stood breathlessly at the door of the mission house. Dr. Price was already there—with Ma-Noo, his housekeeper.

"Marry you!" Mr. Judson was saying. "Are you out of your mind, Jonathan? I can't marry you to this—this Burmese woman. Your good intentions are foolish! You are an American citizen! You have only been in Burma two years; only God knows how long you will be staying. You can't—"

"Adoniram!" Dr. Price interrupted. He pushed Ma-Noo forward gently. "Look at her! She is totally blind, and it's all my fault. If I marry her, I can take care of her—to compensate for my tragic blunder."

Len-Lay felt as if the breath had been knocked

56

out of her. So, it was true! Dr. Price had operated on Ma-Noo—and the operation had failed.

"Oh, Jonathan," spoke up Ann Judson, moving to the housekeeper's side and tenderly putting an arm around her. "Cataract surgery is always risky. You did the best you could. But pity is not a good basis for marriage."

"We will take care of each other. It is the only way," he answered.

Mr. Judson shook his head. "I cannot do it, brother Jonathan. Ma-Noo is not even a believer."

"Not yet," the doctor said stubbornly. "But she is considering what I have told her about Jesus Christ. I am confident she will choose to be baptized." Dr. Price took a deep breath. "Brother Adoniram, I am asking you to perform a wedding. However, the laws of America and nature provide for cases where a minister cannot be found: I will make Ma-Noo my common-law wife!"

In the stunned silence that followed, Len-Lay took the bag of silver ticals from her skirt, laid it on the table, then turned and left the house. Her thoughts and feelings fought wildly with each other as she climbed down from the porch and ran over to the acacia tree in the corner of the vegetable garden that Ann Judson had recently planted. She threw herself down by the tree roots and hugged her knees.

Maybe Myat is right. Maybe Dr. Price is not a real doctor. But even if he isn't, that doesn't mean he is a spy. But why is he pretending? Or maybe he just isn't a very good doctor, she reasoned with herself. *And*

what about the Judsons? They are good people. But
. . . why is Gouger paying them money? Mr. Judson
doesn't work for the young Englishman—so why
should he give them money? Unless—

"Len-Lay?" whispered Mah-Lo, joining her sister under the acacia tree. "Is Myat right? Are the Judsons and Dr. Price spies for the English?"

Len-Lay shook her head. "I—I don't know. I don't think so."

"But what if they are?" insisted Mah-Lo. "Oh, Len-Lay. I'm afraid! What if the emperor hears that Dr. Price made the housekeeper blind? Will he be angry? Will he put all the Americans in prison? What will happen to us? We should never have left Father."

Mr. Judson finally agreed to perform the marriage for Dr. Price and Ma-Noo. Ann Judson helped fix Ma-Noo's hair for the ceremony, winding a wreath of white and pink flowers around the rich, black hair coiled on top of her head. Len-Lay thought the plain-faced housekeeper, with those vacant, unseeing eyes, looked almost pretty as she took Dr. Price's hand and said quietly in Burmese, "I do."

The little group of foreigners—Adoniram and Ann Judson and Henry Gouger—continued to meet at the house of Jonathan and Ma-Noo Price each Sunday for Christian worship, along with Maung Ing, Len-Lay and Mah-Lo. As the rumors of war increased in the city, however, the other curious Burmese quit coming one by one.

As for Mr. Rodgers, who was trying to win back his position in the king's court, he refused to associate with any of the other foreigners in Ava, English *or* American.

One Sunday in late May, the little band of worshipers had just finished saying The Lord's Prayer in Burmese when Koo-Chill, who usually did not attend, burst into the brick house above the river.

"Mr. *Yoodthan!*" gasped the Bengali cook. "I have just heard! The English have attacked and taken Rangoon! Many Burmese have fled the city."

"Rangoon!" everyone cried. Rangoon, on the southern tip of Burma, was the gateway into the rest of the country. If it had fallen, it was only a matter of time until the English sailed up the Irrawaddy River to Ava.

Len-Lay and Mah-Lo looked at each other with fear in their eyes. What about their father? Was Maung Shway-Bay all right?

The hefty cook had finally caught his breath. "General Bandula and his troops are still camped along the Bengali border. The talk in the streets is that General Kyi Wungyi and General Thonby Wungyi are gathering more troops to sail down the Irrawaddy and take Rangoon back. Everyone is saying there will be many white prisoners!"

Henry Gouger shook his head. "Ha! The poor General Wungyis. They have no idea what they're up against."

Mr. Judson frowned. "Henry," he said thoughtfully, "this puts you, as an Englishman, in a bad position. You have a financial interest in Burma and will almost certainly be suspected as a spy. We missionaries, on the other hand, are not here for business or trade; even more important, we are Americans. Our primary safety is keeping our American nationality very clear."

Dr. Price saw what Judson was getting at. "If you are captured, Henry, maybe we can help you from the outside. But if we are seen together, we may all be taken!"

Judson nodded. "I am sorry to say this, Henry. But you must not come to visit us anymore—not until this crisis is over. Please understand, dear friend."

Henry Gouger went to the open door and looked out through the swaying palm trees. The sun was setting over the Irrawaddy River, and it painted the domes and spires of Ava's palaces and temples with fire. "Of course. You are right. This is not the best time to hang around with an Englishman."

The young man forced a smile, turned and blew kisses toward Len-Lay and Mah-Lo. "Goodbye, Princess Mary. Goodbye, Princess Abby. Don't forget your old friend!" Then he was gone.

"Do you really think—?" Mrs. Judson said sadly.

"Yes," said her husband. "I know it seems unkind. But Henry knows I am right; we must not be seen together until the crisis is past. Now . . . we must pray."

After the news from Rangoon, the little mission household tried to go on with life as usual—except that the court official's daughter no longer came for Mrs. Judson's lessons. The workmen continued building the brick house next door to the bamboo *kyuong*. Mr. Judson spent long hours with Maung Ing talking and writing. Sometimes Maung Ing went fishing to keep Koo-Chill's pots full, and Koo-Chill went to the market each day to buy fresh food and listen to the latest war news.

Only a few days later the cook came back with news. "The king's men have arrested Henry Gouger and Mr. Rodgers!" he reported. "Mr. Gouger had a newspaper from India in his house that said that the English government might send an armed fleet against Rangoon. He was arrested for not reporting it to the emperor."

But before the missionaries could do anything to help the Englishmen, Mr. Judson and Dr. Price were themselves summoned before a local judge to answer certain questions. Ann and the girls waited anxiously and were greatly relieved when Mr. Judson returned home that evening.

"What happened?" Mrs. Judson cried.

Mr. Judson shrugged. "The judge said we write many letters. He wanted to know if we were sending reports to foreign countries. Price and I simply told him that we write to friends in the United States—a country thousands of miles away from England. He let us go."

The Judsons hugged. Ann laughed, "Praise God!"

Len-Lay and Mah-Lo, too, relaxed. Maybe nothing bad would happen after all.

But the next evening—Tuesday, June 8—as the little household was sitting down to Koo-Chill's supper, they heard a commotion in the yard, and Mr. Beg Pardon started screeching from his cage on the porch. Then came loud banging on the door. Before Mr. Judson could even get up to open it, the door burst open and a dozen or more Burmese men rushed into the room. Mah-Lo screamed. One of the men had circles branded into his cheeks—the dreaded Spotted Faces! All Burmese had heard of these former criminals—some were missing an ear or a nose or an eye—who became keepers of the prisons. The Spotted Faces were known for treating other prisoners very cruelly.

Another man stepped forward, holding a black book. He wore the turban of a city magistrate, or judge. "Who is the foreign teacher?" he demanded.

"I am," said Mr. Judson, getting up from the table.

"You are under arrest!"

No sooner were the words spoken than the Spotted Face grabbed Mr. Judson and threw him to the floor. Kneeling on his back, he pulled the missionary's arms backward and tied them tightly together at the elbows with a small cord. Mr. Judson winced with pain.

"Stop!" cried Mrs. Judson. "I will give you money—only, please, loosen the cord!"

"Arrest her, too!" snarled the magistrate with the black book.

Without thinking, Len-Lay threw herself at Mrs. Judson, holding her tight. Behind her, Mah-Lo was still crying, held fast in Koo-Chill's big arms. Maung Ing stood horrified at the sight of his American brother bound on the floor.

Mr. Judson struggled to his knees. "Please! Leave my wife alone," he gasped. "I will go with you."

The Spotted Face tightened the cord still further, then dragged Adoniram Judson out of the house, followed by the other men. An anxious crowd had gathered outside, but seeing Mr. Judson being kicked and shoved to the ground, many of the children began crying in fear. The workmen on the brick house had already thrown down their tools and run away.

As the men dragged away her husband, Ann Judson quickly handed a bag of silver ticals to the badly shaken Burmese disciple. "Maung Ing! Follow Mr. Judson. Perhaps you can persuade the Spotted Face to loosen the cord. And tell me where they take him!"

Swallowing his fear, Maung Ing quickly took the money and ran down the street.

Len-Lay was trembling with fear, and Mah-Lo was still weeping in Koo-Chill's arms. Mrs. Judson herded them all inside and bolted the door. Her face was pale but her voice was steady.

"Koo-Chill! Please stand guard at the gate and tell me if anyone comes. Abby, you must stop crying. Mary, both of you can help me. We must work fast."

Following Mrs. Judson's directions, Len-Lay built up the fire that was still smoldering in Koo-Chill's stove. Mrs. Judson and Mah-Lo appeared from the bedroom with handfuls of letters, diaries, and other papers. For almost an hour the woman and two girls fed the fire until nothing remained but ashes.

"Now," she said in a low voice, "take the ashes and scatter them in the garden. We must leave no trace that we have burned anything."

Len-Lay and Mah-Lo scooped the ashes into a large bowl, then cautiously opened the front door. Darkness had fallen, but Koo-Chill's comforting bulk was visible in the moonlight. Without talking, the girls took the ashes to the vegetable garden and scattered them between the rows—just as they did with the ashes from Koo-Chill's fire every day.

As the girls crept quietly back to the house, Len-Lay saw Mrs. Judson climb down from the porch with a thick package under her arm. Picking up a shovel, she disappeared under the house.

While they waited in the house for Mrs. Judson to return, Mah-Lo, still half-crying, stammered, "If—if the Judsons haven't d-done anything wrong, why did Mrs. Judson b-burn all those papers?"

Len-Lay wondered the same thing. And what was in the mysterious package Mrs. Judson was burying under the house?

Len-Lay held her face in her hands. In her mind's eye she could see that terrible Spotted Face twisting Mr. Judson's arms behind his back and dragging him away. She was scared . . . and confused. Why, why, *why* was this happening?

The door opened softly, then closed behind Mrs. Judson, who stood leaning against it a moment, pale and breathless in the semi-darkness. Then she said, "Mary and Abby, we must wash our hands." Using a soft brush in a bowl of water, she gently scrubbed each of the girls' hands, then her own, until there were no traces of ashes or dirt.

As they finished drying their hands, they heard a quiet knock on the door. The girls jumped and clung to Mrs. Judson. Had the Spotted Faces come back? Mrs. Judson put her finger to her lips, shook her head no, then carefully slid back the bolt.

Maung Ing slipped into the house, breathing heavily. Sweat glistened from his face and neck, soaking his tunic. He swallowed several times, then spoke in a choked voice. "Our brother . . . Dr. Price . . . has been arrested, too. I followed. First they were taken to the governor's house, then . . ."

The Burmese disciple paused, his chest heaving.

"*Where*, Maung Ing! Where were they taken!" cried Ann Judson.

Maung Ing finally pushed the words out. "All the white prisoners were taken to . . . the Death Prison!"

Chapter 6

The Death Prison

ANN JUDSON STARED in horror at Maung Ing. For a moment Len-Lay thought her foster mother might faint. But no sooner had Maung Ing said the dreaded words than they heard Koo-Chill, still standing watch at the gate, call out, "Someone is coming!"

Once again there was a loud commotion in the yard, then rough banging on the door. "Mrs. *Yoodthan*, open up!" yelled the magistrate who had been there earlier with his black book. "I must ask you some questions!"

With a quick caution to the girls to say nothing about the papers they had burned, Mrs. Judson closed her eyes briefly, as if breathing a desperate prayer. Then she unbolted the door.

The same official entered, this time alone, though

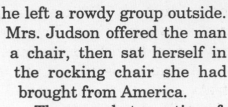

he left a rowdy group outside. Mrs. Judson offered the man a chair, then sat herself in the rocking chair she had brought from America.

The man shot question after question at the foreign woman: Where did she come from? Why had they come to Burma? What were they doing in Ava? Why were these Burmese girls living with them? What religion did they teach? How much money did she have? Who is part of this household? Did she know the Englishman Mr. Henry Gouger? Mr. Rodgers? What was their association? On and on.

Mrs. Judson answered each question calmly. Maung Ing stood behind her; she seemed to draw strength from his presence. Len-Lay and Mah-Lo knelt close at her side.

Finally the magistrate snapped his black book shut and stood up, frowning. "You must not leave this house," he ordered. "I will leave my guard at the gate to make sure you obey." Then he stalked out onto the porch and down the steps into the yard.

Maung Ing watched from the door as the magistrate spoke to the men who had been waiting outside. "Oh, Lord Jesus, preserve us," he muttered. "He has left ten thugs to guard our gates!" With a quick movement, he opened Mr. Beg Pardon's wicker cage, took out the parrot and tossed him into the air to fly up into the surrounding trees.

Mrs. Judson looked alarmed. "Where is Koo-Chill?"

Maung Ing shook his head. "I did not see him. Quick. Bolt the door."

No sooner had the magistrate left than there were loud yells outside and more banging on the door. "Let us in, white lady!" voices called. "Let us in so we can 'protect' you!" followed by rough laughter.

Terrified, Maung Ing, Mrs. Judson, and the two girls pushed the table against the door. Not knowing what else to do, Mrs. Judson then put the girls to bed in her own bed. The girls squeezed their eyes shut, but sleep would not come. The voices outside continued to yell threats and demands that Mrs. Judson unbolt the door.

Then the yelling stopped. Hearing movement in the bedroom, Len-Lay opened her eyes. Mrs. Judson was kneeling beside the bed, her hands clasped, her lips moving silently. Len-Lay knew she was praying.

Suddenly the laughter erupted again, this time from the back of the house, followed by loud groans.

Mrs. Judson cautiously opened the bamboo shutter in the bedroom; Len-Lay crept out of bed and looked out the window beside her. She barely stifled a cry.

Koo-Chill's arms and legs had been fastened in a painful position in a pair of crude stocks; the Bengali servant's face betrayed his distress.

"Stop!" cried Mrs. Judson from the window. "Please let my servant go. I will give each of you money in the morning. But you must let him go now."

The "guards" considered. Back and forth they argued with Mrs. Judson. Finally, they agreed on a price and loosened Koo-Chill from the stocks.

Exhausted, Mrs. Judson and Len-Lay sank down on the bed. They must have slept, because the next thing Len-Lay knew, morning light had brightened the bamboo house.

True to her word, Mrs. Judson gave the ruffians silver ticals the next morning. Koo-Chill, tired, but none the worse for wear after his short ordeal, was let in the house. "Oh, Koo-Chill!" the girls cried, throwing themselves in his big arms. He hugged them, then set about making his fire and cooking a large amount of rice.

Maung Ing nodded his approval. "Burmese custom says that relatives and friends must feed prisoners," he told Mrs. Judson.

"But those—those thugs won't let me out of the

yard!" said Mrs. Judson anxiously.

"We will go," he said, pointing to himself and the two girls.

Len-Lay's eyes widened. *Not to the Death Prison!*

"Yes," said Maung Ing firmly. "Three are better than one: one to talk to guards, one to give food, one to deliver messages—whatever is necessary. They will only allow a few moments. Come. You must be brave. We must work together."

Mrs. Judson didn't want to let the girls go, but Maung Ing finally persuaded her. Even though Len-Lay was scared, she took courage from the boldness Maung Ing was showing. He had always worried about what might happen if Burmese officials discovered he had become a Christian. But now when real danger threatened, he was somehow stronger.

Koo-Chill wrapped rice and several small smoked fish in palm leaves. Mrs. Judson quickly wrote a note to her husband, which Len-Lay tucked into her *longyi*. Then the three messengers stepped out onto the porch.

Mah-Lo noticed the empty cage. "What about Mr. Beg Pardon?" she asked.

With a slight jerk of his head toward the swaying palms overhead, Maung Ing said quietly, "Mr. Beg Pardon is safer up there than in the cage—at least until these no-good ruffians go away."

Most of the "guards" were sleeping off their long, loud night. The two who were awake, however, greedily accepted the gift of silver Maung Ing offered, and let them out the gate. "But not the foreign woman!"

71

one growled, as if to assure himself that he was not neglecting his duty.

It was a two-mile walk through narrow dirt streets to the Death Prison on the far side of Ava. As Maung Ing and the girls drew closer, a terrible smell of unwashed bodies, rotten food, and human waste greeted them. Len-Lay wanted to gag.

"Just breathe through your mouth," Maung Ing said sympathetically.

They found the prison gate, set in a tall bamboo wicket fence with sharp spikes at the top.

"What prisoner?" demanded a guard.

"Adoniram Judson and Jonathan Price, American missionaries," said Maung Ing.

The gate opened and the three were allowed into an outer prison yard. Len-Lay's knees were shaking; she could hear Mah-Lo's rapid breathing. What if— what if those gates closed and they couldn't get out again?

A guard went through a second gate into an inner prison yard. Len-Lay caught a glimpse of a bamboo building with no windows before the gate closed. It was a long time before the inner gate opened again; the guard stepped aside showing two prisoners shuffling behind him.

The girls stared in shock. It was Mr. Judson and Dr. Price. But they were barely recognizable.

Both men had three pairs of iron fetters on each leg connected by short chains. Mr. Judson still had on his black American suit, but it was rumpled and torn and covered with dirt. A bruise was swelling on

Mr. Judson's face where the Spotted Face had struck him on the way to the prison. The hair of both men was matted with dirt, their faces were filthy . . . and they stank.

"God bless you!" blurted Dr. Price.

Mr. Judson opened his mouth but was suddenly overwhelmed with emotion. Silently, he reached out for the food. Len-Lay noticed that his arms seemed stiff and sore.

Maung Ing and the girls piled Koo-Chill's palm leaves full of rice and smoked fish into their hands. Hoping the guard wasn't looking, Len-Lay took Mrs. Judson's note from her *longyi* and slipped it into Mr. Judson's hands.

"Oh, Mary and Abby," he groaned. "I am sorry you had to see this."

"Maung Ing!" whispered Dr. Price. "You must get us out of here. We have been through hell! At night our feet are strung up on a pole and we are hung upside-down, like so many slaughtered sheep—"

"Be quiet, Jonathan!" rasped Mr. Judson, jerking his head toward the girls.

"What about Mr. Gouger and Mr. Rodgers?" Maung Ing asked.

"They are alive—"

"Enough!" yelled the guard behind them. "You have your food. Visitors must go." He jerked the prisoners away from the inner gate, locked it, then escorted Maung Ing and the girls across the outer yard and pushed them outside.

Myat Rodgers was standing outside the prison gate, holding a bundle of food, looking frightened.

"Did you see my father?" he asked anxiously.

"No, young son," Maung Ing said gently. "But he is still alive."

Myat's face clouded angrily. "*Why* is my father in the Death Prison! He is a loyal Burmese citizen! It is the other foreigners' fault." The boy glared accusingly at Len-Lay and Mah-Lo. "One of them is a spy—or maybe all of them! But now the king trusts no one—not even my father. It's not fair! He has served the royal house for forty years—and look how badly he is treated!"

Len-Lay and Mah-Lo, still upset by what they had seen inside the prison yard, hardly knew how to respond to Myat's outburst. But Len-Lay felt sorry for him, in spite of his angry accusations. If Mr. Rodgers looked as bad as Mr. Judson and Dr. Price, Myat was in for a shock.

"The king's men even came to our house and looked through all my father's papers," Myat stormed. "But they didn't find anything—not like that Gouger fellow."

"What do you mean?" Maung Ing asked quickly.

Myat smiled triumphantly. "You'll find out soon enough. They'll come to your house, too."

"Oh, but we bur—ow!" Mah-Lo had started to tell Myat that they'd burned all Judson's papers, but was silenced by a swift kick from Len-Lay.

"No one is a spy, young son," Maung Ing said hastily. "The government will soon realize your father and all these men are innocent and will release them. Now . . . you had better deliver that food to your father. Seeing you will be food for his spirit, as well."

The anger faded from Myat's eyes and the fear returned. Without another word he marched to the prison gate. As Maung Ing and the girls started the two-mile trek back to the mission house, they heard the guard snap: "What prisoner?" and Myat, his voice wavering only slightly, replied: "Rodgers, known as Yadza, Burmese citizen."

The magistrate with the black book was at the house when Maung Ing and the girls returned. He did not say anything about other members of the household being absent, as long as Mrs. Judson did not escape.

"Please, let me go into Ava to see the city governor," Mrs. Judson pleaded. "My husband is innocent. I must plead his case."

"No," said the magistrate stubbornly. "My orders are to keep you here."

"At least tell me why my husband has been put in prison," Mrs. Judson insisted. "What are the charges?"

"We are still investigating. But it looks bad for your husband. We know for a fact that he has been receiving money from the English. Why else would they pay him wages—unless he has been working for them as a spy?"

"What?" said Mrs. Judson. "What do you mean? We receive no money from the English."

"But that is not true, gracious lady," the magistrate smirked. "The young trader, Mr. Gouger, has been giving you money regularly. We have proof—"

Len-Lay did not wait to hear any more. She grabbed Mah-Lo's arm and pulled her out of the house. Ignoring Mah-Lo's protests, Len-Lay half-dragged her sister toward the garden. The rowdy men guarding the gate made crude remarks as the girls passed, but Len-Lay didn't think they would do anything as long as the magistrate was in the house.

Once the girls had reached the acacia tree, Len-Lay whirled on her sister. "Did you hear what that man said?" she demanded.

"Y-yes," stammered Mah-Lo.

"You and your big mouth!" Len-Lay said angrily. "You told Myat that Mr. Gouger had given us money for the Judsons. He must have told someone—because that's why they arrested Mr. Judson."

Len-Lay was breathing hard, and she shook Mah-Lo by the shoulders. "Don't you understand what has happened? It's *our fault* that Mr. Judson is in the Death Prison!"

Chapter 7

The Hard Pillow

MAH-LO PULLED AWAY from her older sister, avoiding her eyes, her lip trembling. Then she lifted her head and stuck out her chin stubbornly. "It is *not* my fault. I didn't know it was a bad thing for Mr. Gouger to give money to the Judsons."

"Maybe it was, and maybe it wasn't! We still don't know," Len-Lay argued.

"What do you mean, 'we don't know'? The magistrate said Mr. Gouger paid Mr. Judson to be a spy for the English," Mah-Lo reminded her.

"That's what *he* said." Then Len-Lay fell silent. Again her thoughts and feelings played tug-of-war inside her, and the lump in her throat returned. Finally she said, "Do you think Mr. Judson should be in the Death Prison?"

Mah-Lo looked shocked. "No! Of course not."

"Do you think he is a spy?" Len-Lay pushed.

"I . . ." Mah-Lo looked at the ground. "I don't know."

The magistrate was leaving the mission yard. Miserably, Len-Lay walked back to the house, with Mah-Lo trailing behind her.

"Remember!" the man called up to Mrs. Judson, who was standing in the open door. "We will be back to make a list of all your property and household goods. A prisoner no longer has any possessions; they are now the property of the king!"

There were no school lessons that day; Mrs. Judson was too troubled. She spent long hours in the bedroom praying, or pacing about the house, lost in thought. The girls barely talked to each other, either. All Len-Lay could think was: *Is it our fault?*

As evening fell, Mrs. Judson again promised presents and silver ticals to the rowdy men outside, if they would not bother them that night. It worked; even though the men built a bonfire in the mission yard and laughed rudely among themselves, there were no threats or banging on the door. Again, Mrs. Judson let the girls crawl into her own bed where they slept, exhausted.

The next morning, Maung Ing was sent across the river to fetch Dr. Price's blind wife, Ma-Noo, and bring her to the mission house. In the meantime, Koo-Chill cooked a big pot of curried chicken that he wrapped in palm leaves.

The magistrate came early to be sure that Mrs.

79

Judson was still under house arrest. This time she begged him to take a note to the city governor, saying she wanted to visit him so she might give him a present. Grudgingly, the man agreed to deliver the note . . . and returned a few hours later with permission for Mrs. Judson to visit the governor that afternoon.

By the time Maung Ing had returned with Ma-Noo, the guards did not want to let someone new into the mission yard, but the magistrate—after thinking about it—decided that the wife of the other American missionary would then be his "prisoner" as well. The poor woman had not wanted to leave her own home, but she also had no way to get news or send food and supplies to Dr. Price. So in the end, she had agreed to come.

When Ma-Noo heard that Mrs. Judson was going to see the city governor, she said, "Mrs. *Yoodthan*, my friend. Take off your American clothes and dress as a Burmese woman. It will tell the governor that you are indeed a friend of Burma."

Ann Judson had been given a beautiful royal blue *longyi* and short tunic with a matching silk scarf by the wife of one of the court officials. After dressing and adjusting the scarf over her shoulders, Mrs. Judson asked Len-Lay to help fix her hair, which she normally wore in a bun at the nape of her neck.

Len-Lay combed Mrs. Judson's dark brown hair up on top of her head, Burmese style, but try as she might, she could not capture all the little curls that escaped and framed her foster mother's face. But a few flowers from the garden tucked around the coil on top of her head gave the desired effect.

Mrs. Judson looked beautiful.

Then Len-Lay noticed Mrs. Judson's shoes—sturdy, black American footwear. "Oh, no," Mrs. Judson protested noticing the girls' disapproval. "I will change my dress, but not my shoes."

The little group decided that Maung Ing and Len-Lay should go with Mrs. Judson, and take the food for the prisoners. This time Koo-Chill included some fruit and a pot of tea.

At the governor's palace, Mrs. Judson bowed low and gave the elderly governor a dinner plate with a picture of the White House in Washington, D.C., America, etched on it. The gift delighted him. The old man, obviously enchanted by this beautiful foreign woman, then listened patiently as she made her request.

"O wise one," she said, "all the foreigners have

been put in the Death Prison. The Spotted Faces treat them badly. But the teacher and the doctor, at least, are from America—a country many thousands of miles away from England. They have nothing to do with this war between Burma and England."

The governor stroked his long chin beard. "I cannot remove them from the prison. But they can be made more comfortable. Here—speak to my head officer. He will tell you what can be done."

As it turned out, the head officer demanded a large bribe before he would do anything to help the prisoners. Again, Ann Judson found herself bargaining back and forth until the man finally agreed: two hundred ticals of silver—about one hundred American dollars—and two pieces of fine cloth. In return, the officer gave Mrs. Judson a palm leaf with written instructions on it.

As the trio neared the Death Prison, Mrs. Judson was dismayed by the terrible smell. Len-Lay dreaded going in that awful place again, but she tried to be brave. She could feel Mrs. Judson trembling as the Spotted Face opened the first gate and led them across to the inner prison gate.

Someone else was there delivering food to a prisoner. Len-Lay recognized one of Gouger's servants, then realized Gouger himself was standing just beyond the inner gate.

"Oh, Mrs. Judson," he said miserably. "I do not wish to have you see me like this." Henry Gouger shuffled away with his ration of food as fast as his chains would allow.

Mrs. Judson was mute, as if trying her best to ignore the iron fetters and filthy condition of their friend. She kept her eyes fixed on the windowless bamboo house just beyond the gate. After a long time, a figure appeared at the door—*crawling*.

It was Adoniram Judson.

Mrs. Judson gave a little cry, then buried her face in her hands. She swayed and almost fell, but Len-Lay slipped an arm around Mrs. Judson's slim waist and steadied her.

As Mr. Judson crawled toward the gate, Maung Ing stepped forward and helped him stand up. With a slight shudder, Mrs. Judson put down her hands and looked her husband in the face. With a great effort she smiled.

"Oh, Ann," he whispered through cracked and swollen lips. "It is wonderful to see you. But, please . . . don't come here."

"I have orders from the governor to make you more comfortable," she said, handing the palm-leaf message to the guard.

The Spotted Face glanced at the note. "Get out," he snarled.

"But—"

"Get out!"

Maung Ing and Len-Lay quickly handed the food and tea to Mr. Judson before the Spotted Face roughly herded them outside the prison walls. No one spoke as they trudged the two miles toward home.

Len-Lay was miserable. *What if it really was*

83

their fault that Mr. Judson was in the Death Prison?
The thought lay like a stone in her stomach.

The magistrate returned and went through the house with Mrs. Judson. He took several things he thought were "nice" or "valuable," and made a list of everything else. But when he went away this time, he took the ruffians with him. The governor had sent orders that Ann Judson should be free to come and go as she pleased.

And on his next visit to the prison, Maung Ing reported that Mrs. Judson's efforts must have succeeded, because the foreign prisoners had been moved out of the terrible torture house where their chained feet had been lifted each night by a long pole until only their shoulders touched the floor. Now they slept in an open shed in the inner prison yard. The shed wasn't much, but at least they could lie flat and the air moved freely.

The whole household felt like cheering. Only one thing puzzled them. Mr. Beg Pardon had not returned.

Every other day Mrs. Judson went to the governor's house to plead her husband's case. She did this graciously, sipping tea and talking with various members of his household. On alternate days, she visited other important officials in the city, asking them if they would speak to the king on the missionaries' behalf. As Ma-Noo had suggested, she now only wore Burmese dress, much to the delight of the Burmans. Most listened politely, but shook their heads. "We can do nothing."

Many summer mornings Mrs. Judson was ill, sometimes vomiting and staying in bed until nearly noon. The constant worry and endless efforts to free the prisoners were draining her strength. She relied often on Maung Ing, Len-Lay, and Mah-Lo to visit the Death Prison with food, fresh clothes, and messages.

The news they brought back to the mission house varied from day to day. Sometimes the prisoners were in good spirits; sometimes, when the Burmese army suffered a defeat, they were dragged back to the torture house. It took *more* visits to government officials and *more* bribes to gain each small favor.

As the long, hot summer months finally turned into fall, Mrs. Judson's strength seemed to return. One day she went to the Death Prison to visit Adoniram by herself. When she returned, she cut up one of her old brown American skirts and began sewing two large rectangles of cloth together. The girls watched curiously, but since Mrs. Judson didn't offer an explanation, they didn't ask.

When darkness fell and the girls were lying on Mrs. Judson's bed, restless in the still night air, they heard their foster mother leave the house. After a few minutes, they heard the soft *chink, chink* of a shovel digging underneath the house.

"She's burying something else under the house!" Mah-Lo whispered.

"Or digging something up," Len-Lay whispered back. The older girl tiptoed to the bedroom door and peeked into the main room just in time to see Mrs. Judson come back in with a large package—it looked like the one she had buried before. Mrs. Judson placed the package inside the cloth bag, then began stuffing scraps of the old skirt in around it.

Len-Lay crept back to bed and felt all the confusion return. *Should she trust the Judsons or expose them?* All night her thoughts went back and forth.

The next morning it was obvious what Mrs. Judson had been making: an uncomfortable-looking, brown pillow.

"Adoniram asked me to bring him a pillow that was so hard and ugly that none of the Spotted Faces would steal it!" she smiled. "But I have to visit the queen's sister-in-law today. She is my one last hope to present a plea to the king. Mary and Abby, would you go with Maung Ing when he delivers food to the prison today, and take the pillow to Mr. Judson?"

Len-Lay hesitated. She

wanted to ask what was inside the pillow, but did not dare. *What if a Spotted Face grabbed it and ripped it apart? What if—*

But Mrs. Judson's eyes were pleading. *Please. Take the pillow.* Len-Lay finally nodded. If it was their fault that Mr. Judson had been arrested, the least she could do was swallow her fear and take the pillow to him.

But Mah-Lo shook her head. "No! I have a stomachache. I want to stay home with Ma-Noo and Koo-Chill. Besides—I hate going to the Death Prison! I don't want to go anymore!" And Mah-Lo ran from the room and threw herself onto the bed.

Len-Lay stared after her sister, then said quickly, "That's all right. Maung Ing and I can carry the food and the pillow by ourselves."

As the Burmese man and young girl neared the Death Prison, Len-Lay worried. The pillow was very heavy; surely the Spotted Faces would know something was inside. Sweat trickled down her back.

Myat Rodgers was standing outside the prison gate, waiting for the guards to let him in with food for his father. *Oh, no!* Len-Lay panicked. *Myat will certainly guess that we are smuggling something inside this pillow. He is so suspicious.* She tried to carry the pillow carelessly, as if it was nothing. But it felt heavier with every step.

But Myat hardly seemed to notice them. His shoulders sagged, and his eyes studied the dirt at his feet.

"How is your father, the honorable Mr. Rodgers?"

said Maung Ing kindly.

For a moment Myat didn't say anything. Then he looked at them dully. "My father is going crazy. He is sure that the Spotted Faces are going to torture and kill him. Every day he asks me to bring him poison, so that he can kill himself first. But my mother will not send it."

Len-Lay did not move, but inside she wanted to reach out and touch Myat, to let him know she understood. Right now he did not seem like the proud, taunting boy she'd first met; he was confused and scared.

"Your mother is right," said Maung Ing gently. "You must always hold on to hope."

"But the war is not going well," Myat muttered. "Haven't you heard? The English have defeated both General Kyi Wungyi and General Thonby Wungyi. The Redcoat soldiers are slowly marching toward Ava. Soon we may all be prisoners of war—or dead!"

Chapter 8

A Cry in the Night

INSTEAD OF GOING to get the prisoners, two Spotted Faces appeared at the gate and gruffly took the drab pillow and the food for Mr. Judson and Mr. Rodgers. Myat seemed almost relieved that he didn't have to go inside. But Len-Lay knew this meant the foreign prisoners had been chained inside the torture house again.

When Maung Ing and Len-Lay got back to the mission house, Mrs. Judson had just returned from a visit to the Princess of Sarawaddy. But the bad news from the war front had the whole city of Ava in a sour mood. The little household encouraged Mrs. Judson to stay home for a few days rather than risk getting a flat "No" to her request for the prisoners' release.

"Why did you refuse to go with us to the Death Prison?" Len-Lay asked her sister. They had finished supper and were sitting alone on the porch under Mr. Beg Pardon's empty cage. Each evening they sat peering into the treetops, hoping to catch a glimpse of the pet parrot.

But tonight Mah-Lo was sullen. "I delivered the spy money to Mr. Judson, but I'm not going to deliver a spy pillow."

"Stupid girl!" Len-Lay scowled. "You don't know that it was a spy pillow!"

"You don't know that it wasn't!" Mah-Lo shot back. "Mrs. Judson was smuggling *something* in that pillow; you and I both know *that*. What if we got caught with it? Then we would all be put in the Death Prison!"

Len-Lay nodded. "Yes, I was very afraid," she admitted.

Mah-Lo stared at her. "You were? Then why did you go?"

"Because . . ." Len-Lay stopped. Why *had* she gone? Somewhere in the back of her mind she remembered their reading lesson that came from the Christian Bible: "For God so loved the world, that he gave his only begotten Son . . ." The Judsons were like that; they had given up everything. She didn't understand everything they did, but they loved Burma and the Burmese people. And everything was so scary and confusing right now, that she had to trust *somebody*.

But she didn't know how to explain this to Mah-Lo.

✦ ✦ ✦ ✦

Ann Judson was restless, unable to do anything to help the prisoners. After a week had gone by, she decided to take the girls and risk another visit to the Princess of Sarawaddy and ask—discreetly—if the princess had talked to her sister-in-law, the queen. Mrs. Judson dressed the girls in their most beautiful silk *longyis* and embroidered blouses; she, however, borrowed one of Ma-Noo's roomy tunics that, Len-Lay thought privately, made her look rather dumpy.

The palace of the queen's brother and his wife had a beautiful courtyard with a pool of cool water in the center. Two peacocks, one a brilliant blue-green and the other white, strutted slowly along the glossy tiles, dragging their long tail feathers on the ground.

Mah-Lo's mouth fell open and she gaped at the fine furnishings. Len-Lay tried to act casual, but she, too, was tempted to stare.

They waited nearly half an hour for the princess, but when a servant finally ushered them into her private sitting room, Len-Lay was amazed at how cool it felt. The thick stone walls of the palace kept out the muggy heat of early fall—much different from their bamboo *kyuong*.

The princess wore bright scarlet, indicating royalty. Her bright red lips, the red combs and jewels in her hair, gave her a rosy glow like the sunset. Like most Burmese women, she was shorter than Mrs. Judson, but she stood slim and straight.

Mrs. Judson and the girls *sheekoed* politely. The

princess bowed in return. "It is I who am honored by a visit from the wife of the foreign teacher," she said.

Len-Lay's heart thumped. That was a good sign. At least the Judsons were respected in this household.

Another servant brought cool fruit drinks. The two women sat on a cushioned bench and chatted back and forth in Burmese, while the girls squatted nearby on a beautifully painted mat, sipping the sweet mango juice. During a brief lull in the conversation, Mrs. Judson asked, "O lady of ruby reds, did you present my request to the queen?"

Princess Sarawaddy looked down at her slim brown hands, covered with gold rings and jewels. "I did." After a moment, she lifted her eyes and looked sadly at Mrs. Judson. "The queen said the foreign prisoners will not be killed, but they must stay in the Death Prison."

Mrs. Judson's shoulders sagged. Sympathetically, the princess laid her brown hand over the other woman's white one. "Your condition is advancing. Are you well? Can I do something to help you if your husband is not released by the time the little one is born?"

The princess's words startled the two girls. Both of them stared at their foster mother. Mrs. Judson was going to have a *baby*?

She should have known, Len-Lay chided herself later. There were many mornings when Mrs. Judson had been sick . . . and lately she'd been borrowing those large tunics from Ma-Noo. Burmese women talked openly about these things, but Mrs. Judson had said nothing. Len-Lay shook her head. Foreign women had many strange ways.

But Ann Judson's pregnancy soon became obvious to everyone—even to Adoniram's red, suffering eyes. "Oh, Ann," he moaned next time visitors were allowed. "How useless I feel; I can't be of help to you. Why didn't you tell me sooner?"

"I did not want to add

to your worries, beloved," his wife said gently.

Len-Lay, who had accompanied Mrs. Judson that day, looked away, trying to give her foster parents a moment of privacy. As she looked around, trying not to smell the foul air or see the rats roaming freely around the prison yard, she realized that she had not seen Myat for a couple of weeks.

"When will the baby be born?" she heard Mr. Judson ask in his tired voice.

"Early February—I think," murmured Mrs. Judson.

Len-Lay saw one of the Spotted Faces coming. Quickly, she turned back to Mr. Judson. "Has Myat Rodgers come to see his father lately?" she asked.

A troubled look crossed Mr. Judson's face. "No, Mary. In fact, no one has brought Mr. Rodgers any food recently. We have been sharing ours with him."

"Enough!" shouted the Spotted Face. "Out! Out! This isn't a tea party!" Within moments, the guards rudely pushed Len-Lay and Mrs. Judson out the gate.

All the way home Len-Lay worried. What had happened to Myat? Maung Ing had gone fishing, so she mentioned her concern to Koo-Chill.

"Go and see, then," said the cook impatiently. The months of cooking for the prisoners on top of his regular duties had made him more upset recently— though he never showed it to Mrs. Judson. "And take Abby with you. I'm tired of looking at her pouting face."

Mrs. Judson was resting, so Len-Lay talked Mah-

Lo into going with her to the Rodgers' big house. The two girls trudged silently to the section of Ava where most of the city officials lived. The Rodgers' house seemed unusually quiet, but Len-Lay pulled the bell rope and they heard the bell clanging inside.

The girls waited several minutes and were just about to give up and turn away when the door opened a crack. An eye peered out at them, then the door opened a few more inches.

It was Myat.

Len-Lay smiled. "Oh, Myat! I'm so glad it's you. We—er—were kind of worried because we hadn't seen you at the prison for a while."

Myat just looked at them through the small gap in the door.

"Well, let us in!" Mah-Lo demanded. "We've come to see you. Don't leave us out here in the street."

The door opened wider; Myat turned without a word and walked back into the small courtyard in the center of the house. The girls followed. No servants were in sight.

"Are you all right, Myat?" Len-Lay asked. "Has something happened?"

Myat nodded. He looked around at the empty house. A muscle under his left eyelid twitched.

"The magistrate came and . . . took all our household property. He said that everything belonged to the king, now. My—my mother didn't know what to do. Her relatives came to get her. They said the family was . . . disgraced because her English husband was a—a traitor. She wanted to take me, but I knew they . . . didn't want me." Myat drew a long, shaky breath. "Because I am . . . half English."

Len-Lay stared. "You mean, you are all alone here?"

Myat nodded. "The servants left, too. And I—I have no food to take to my father. Now . . . he will die." The boy turned his head away from the girls.

"No! No . . . he will not die," said Len-Lay. "Mr. Judson and Dr. Price are sharing their food with him—and probably Henry Gouger, too."

Myat turned and stared at the girls. "Why? Why would they do that?" His eyes dropped to the floor. "My father refused to help *them*."

"Maung Ing told me once that the followers of Jesus Christ were supposed to love their enemies," Mah-Lo blurted.

"Mr. Rodgers is not an enemy," Len-Lay scolded.

Mah-Lo shrugged.

"But what about you?" Len-Lay asked Myat. "You must come back to the mission house with us. Koo-Chill will be glad to give you some food." *I think*, she added to herself.

Myat shook his head and pulled himself up. "No. I'm no beggar boy. I'll get by."

The girls were quiet on the way home, each thinking her separate thoughts. It was Mah-Lo who finally broke the silence—and her thoughts had not been about Myat Rodgers.

"Mary," she said slowly, "when Mrs. Judson has her own baby to take care of . . . do you think she will want us anymore?"

Len-Lay stopped and looked at her sister. She almost said, *Of course!* But something held her back. If Mrs. Judson had a baby, maybe she wouldn't have time to teach Burmese girls to read and write anymore. And when Maung Shway-Bay had brought his daughters to the Judsons, Ann Judson had said "Yes" because her own arms were empty. But what if those arms had a baby in them?

"I don't know," she finally said, taking Mah-Lo's hand. "We will have to wait and see. What else can we do?"

Koo-Chill came home from the market with news: The king had sent for General Bandula to come back from the Bengali border. Suddenly the mood of the city changed. General Bandula would turn those Redcoats back! General Bandula would rout the English from Rangoon! General Bandula was going to save Burma! By the time the general marched through Ava on his way to Rangoon in October, he was already a hero.

It was good news for the prisoners, as well. Once more the city governor listened when Mrs. Judson pled for better treatment of the prisoners, sweetening her request with presents.

"One of these days the magistrate is going to come back with his list—but many things will be missing!" Len-Lay told her sister, giggling.

A few more bribes and the foreign prisoners were taken out of the torture house once again and each

97

given a little shed in the inner yard of the prison. The guards allowed Mrs. Judson to spend an hour or two at a time visiting with her husband in his own shed.

But as her pregnancy progressed, Ann's visits became fewer. She seemed worn out and often lay, listless, on the bed. Koo-Chill was constantly trying to tempt her with food, but sometimes all she would eat was a savory soup or broth.

Ma-Noo kept the girls busy helping her mend clothes for the household and making some necessary things for the baby. Many of Ann Judson's American clothes disappeared and reappeared made into a small blanket or shirt.

Maung Ing and Len-Lay made the daily trips to the prison. When Mr. Judson asked how Ann was, Maung Ing would grin widely and say, "Mrs. *Yoodthan* says to tell you the baby is kicking her like a mule-rider!" or "Mrs. *Yoodthan* sends her love!" Len-Lay wondered if Mr. Judson ever realized that Maung Ing was evading his question.

November and December of 1824 passed with the same dreary routines. In spite of Mrs. Judson's poor health, she managed to keep teaching the girls their lessons, using short passages from the Bible, written out in Burmese on a sheet of paper, for practice in reading and writing.

At the end of December, they heard one *boom!* from a signal cannon on the river. That meant bad news. General Bandula's main attack had failed, and the English were driving him and his seven thousand men back in retreat.

Mr. Judson had now been a prisoner for eight months. Mrs. Judson wanted to go see him, to encourage him, but Maung Ing and Koo-Chill were firm: She must save her strength for the birth of the child.

One night in late January, a strange sound awoke Len-Lay. She sat up on her pallet at the foot of Mrs. Judson's bed and listened. There it was again: a long, low groan.

Instantly, Len-Lay scrambled to the side of the bed. Mrs. Judson was breathing hard and her hair was damp with sweat. "Get Ma-Noo—"

Len-Lay woke up everybody. "Quick! Quick! The baby is coming."

Ma-Noo immediately parked herself next to Mrs. Judson, wringing out damp cloths and bathing her sweaty body. She loosened Mrs. Judson's clothing and massaged her abdomen gently. Her sightless face broke into a small smile. "The baby's head is down; good."

Everyone waited expectantly, the silence broken only by Mrs. Judson's heavy breathing and the deep groans about every ten minutes. But hours went by; the sun came up and nothing had happened. Koo-Chill made something to eat, but no one was hungry.

Maung Ing began pacing back and forth in the main room. "She is too worn out!" Maung Ing worried. "The baby will not come!"

"Out!" Koo-Chill ordered. "Take rice to the prison, but don't talk to Mr. Judson today. Do you understand? Say nothing!"

The Bengali cook then moved into the bedroom. "I will be your eyes, Ma-Noo," he said gently. "Tell me what to do."

"We must lift her up," said the blind woman. "She does not have the strength. But she must be upright so the baby can come down."

Tenderly, the big man helped Mrs. Judson into a squatting position. She was so weak that her full weight leaned against him, her head rolling back on his shoulder. Frightened, Len-Lay and Mah-Lo watched from the doorway.

Slowly the sun traveled its arc in the sky, then sank behind the spires of the golden pagodas. Sometimes Ma-Noo or Koo-Chill came out of the bedroom for a brief rest. The girls quickly fetched fresh, cool water or clean cloths whenever they were asked; otherwise they crouched right outside the bedroom door. Maung Ing, however, paced outside in the yard, praying to Jesus Christ.

The house darkened. Candles were lit. Almost twenty hours had gone by since Len-Lay first woke up the household. Suddenly Mrs. Judson's face screwed up for one final, great effort.

"Yes, yes. Now push him out," coached Ma-Noo soothingly. "Push! Push!"

The groans turned into screams. Len-Lay and Mah-Lo clutched each other outside the door and buried their faces. On and on went Mrs. Judson's cries, punctuated by Ma-Noo's commands: "Push! Push!"

And then, suddenly, everything was quiet. Too quiet.

Then they heard Ma-Noo's soft, urgent voice. "Cry, little one! Cry!"

Maung Ing stood wide-eyed looking into the house from the porch. Len-Lay shook her head at him; she didn't know what was happening.

Then Mah-Lo's fingers dug into Len-Lay's arm. They heard it coming from the bedroom: a long, thin cry.

A baby's cry!

Chapter 9

Disappeared

Maung Ing heard the baby's cry, too. He rushed to the two girls and wrapped them in a joyful hug. "Praise to God the Father!" he cried, tears spilling down his face. "The baby lives!"

Koo-Chill came to the bedroom door. A tired smile cracked his wide face. "Come in—just for a moment," he said to the girls. "Mrs. *Yoodthan* is asking for you."

Timidly, Len-Lay and Mah-Lo entered the tiny room. Mrs. Judson was lying on the bed, her dark hair loose and wet on the pillow. Tucked in the crook of her arm was the baby, wrapped in one of Ma-Noo's homemade blankets, and sucking on its fist.

Mrs. Judson smiled weakly. With difficulty she gathered up the tiny bundle and held it out to Len-

Lay. "Mary and Abby," she whispered, "I want you to meet your new baby sister . . . Maria Elizabeth."

Len-Lay looked at Mah-Lo and their eyes both said the same thing: *She called the baby our little sister!*

Len-Lay took the bundle and sat on the edge of the bed. Mah-Lo pulled away the blanket for a better look. The baby had not even been washed yet; she was thin and white, and not very pretty. But Len-Lay kissed her softly on the forehead before handing the baby back to Mrs. Judson.

Mrs. Judson slept all the rest of the night and most of the next day and night, except for nursing little Maria. The next day Maung Ing and Len-Lay delivered the good news to Mr. Judson in the prison.

"He is so happy, Mrs. *Yoodthan*!" Maung Ing reported, beaming. "He says he cannot wait until he can see you and baby Maria. He says you must rest and get your strength back."

What Maung Ing didn't tell Mrs. Judson—Len-Lay knew—was that, at the news that his wife and child were both alive, Mr. Judson had covered his face with his hands—and cried.

On the second day Mrs. Judson sat up in bed, sipping Koo-Chill's delicious broth. Mah-Lo sat cross-legged on the bed at her feet, cuddling the sleeping baby. Len-Lay knelt beside her foster mother, brushing her rich, dark hair.

"Sweet Mary! Dear Abby!" Mrs. Judson said, setting down her empty bowl. "You have been such a comfort to me. Do you think . . . would you please call me Mama Ann—instead of Mrs. Judson?"

Len-Lay stopped brushing. Mah-Lo looked startled.

"Of course we will honor Mah-Kyi and Maung Shway-Bay as your birth parents," Mrs. Judson said hastily. "But since we are your second family, maybe . . . you could call us Mama Ann and Papa 'Don?" Mrs. Judson looked uncertainly from one girl to the other.

Suddenly Mah-Lo laid the baby down, threw herself into Mrs. Judson's arms and burst into tears. It was Mrs. Judson's turn to be startled.

"Oh, my, oh, my," she said, holding the sobbing Mah-Lo. "I didn't mean to upset you, Abby. We can forget the whole thing."

"Ohhh, Mrs. Judson," wailed the younger girl. "You wouldn't want me at all if you knew what I've done!" And she cried all the harder.

Mrs. Judson looked at Len-Lay, perplexed. "Mary, whatever is she talking about?"

Len-Lay's mouth suddenly felt dry. Gripping the hairbrush and swallowing hard, she finally said in a near-whisper, "You see, Mrs. Judson, it is our fault that Mr. Judson was put into prison."

Ann Judson's eyes widened. "Whatever are you talking about! Of course it isn't—"

Now that Len-Lay had started, the words just kept tumbling out. "Don't you remember the day Mr. Judson sent us to Mr. Gouger's house with a note? And—and Mr. Gouger gave us money to bring back to Mr. Judson."

Mrs. Judson frowned and nodded.

"Well, Myat Rodgers met us on the way home and wanted to know what we were doing. Mah-Lo—Abby—told him about the money. But she didn't mean to! We didn't know Mr. Judson would be arrested for taking money from the Englishman! Myat must have told someone—because—because then the horrible Spotted Faces came for Mr. Judson! And—and we overheard the magistrate tell you Mr. Gouger must be paying Mr. Judson to be a spy!"

Now Len-Lay threw herself on her face in Mrs. Judson's lap. "Oh, Mrs. *Yoodthan*!" she cried, also bursting into tears. "Now you will hate us and send us away—forever!"

The secret was out. Both Len-Lay and Mah-Lo shook with sobs. Then Len-Lay felt Mrs. Judson's hands lifting her up.

"Hush, now, both of you," she said firmly. "Look at me."

Gradually the sobbing ceased. Len-Lay and Mah-Lo sat up, but kept their eyes downcast. Mrs. Judson lifted their chins. "Mary and Abby. Look at me."

The girls finally lifted their eyes.

"Listen carefully," said Mrs. Judson. "It is true that Mr. Judson was arrested because the government found out that Henry Gouger was giving us money. But that is *not* your fault! The magistrate took all Mr. Gouger's account books, and there it was all written down: so much money to Mr. Judson this month, so much the next month, and so on. Do you understand? He found out because Mr. Gouger wrote it in his books—*not* because you told Myat."

It took several moments for Mrs. Judson's words to sink in. Then relief washed over Len-Lay like a cool bath. Mrs. Judson was not angry. She did not blame them. It was not their fault.

"B-but, what about the money?" Mah-Lo stammered. Len-Lay knew what she was asking: Was it spy money?

Mrs. Judson gave a short laugh. "I tried to explain to the magistrate, but he wouldn't listen. Mr. Gouger was simply cashing checks for us."

Both girls looked at her blankly. What did cashing checks mean?

Maria Elizabeth was starting to squirm. Mrs. Judson picked up the baby and patted her back. "You see," Mrs. Judson went on, "it's not very safe to send money in a letter. So when the mission board in America collects money for our support, they put it in a bank and send us a check—a piece of paper saying how much money they are sending. We are supposed to give the check to a bank here, and the bank is supposed to give us the money. Then the bank would collect from the American bank later."

"But," puzzled Len-Lay, "there are no banks in Burma."

"Exactly," said Mrs. Judson wryly. "So we gave our checks to Mr. Gouger and *he* gave us the money. Then he sent the checks to his bank in England—"

Maria Elizabeth interrupted with a lusty yell, and Mrs. Judson gave up trying to explain about banks. The girls scrambled off the bed. But at the door Mah-Lo turned back and blew two kisses.

"One for Maria," she said with a shy smile, "and one for Mama Ann."

The baby was twenty days old before Mrs. Judson was strong enough to walk to the prison. Maung Ing and both girls went with her carrying as much rice, vegetables, and fruit as Koo-Chill could barter for.

Mr. Judson was haggard and his ragged clothes hung on his bones. But taking his infant daughter into his arms, his face lighted up. The baby was tiny, but her strong fist waved in his face. Two or three Spotted Faces even looked their way curiously; they had never seen a baby so pale and white. The following day Maung Ing brought a poem that Mr. Judson had written in his little shed in the prison yard.

Mrs. Judson unfolded the small piece of paper and tenderly read the words aloud.

Sleep, darling infant, sleep,
  Hushed on thy mother's breast;
Let no rude sound of clanking chains
  Disturb thy balmy rest.

But two weeks later, the guards at the prison roughly told the little family that they couldn't see Mr. Judson. All foreign prisoners had been put back inside the torture house. Ann Judson marched straight to the house of the city governor.

"Don't ask me for any more favors!" said the old man. "Go away. I cannot help you anymore."

But Mrs. Judson was persistent. Within a few days she was back, her infant child and the two Burmese girls at her side, begging the governor to let the prisoners out into the yard.

"You do not know what you are asking!" cried the governor. "The king's brother strongly implied that the prisoners should be killed. I have moved them inside the prison house—out of sight—to save their lives." The old man looked as if he would cry. "Now go away! Stay home, if you value your husband's life."

Len-Lay knew that her foster mother was really frightened now for her husband's life. She busied herself at home, caring for Maria Elizabeth, and helping the girls with their lessons. But each day when Maung Ing came back from delivering food to the prison, she asked eagerly for any word from her husband. There was none.

February dragged by, and then it was March. Mr. Beg Pardon's cage still hung, empty, from the porch roof. Every time the girls looked at it, they felt sad. And no word had come from the Rangoon mission since the English had captured the coastal city. Why didn't they get a letter? Was their father, Maung Shway-Bay, dead or alive? Would they ever see him again?

Twice when Len-Lay took food to the prison with Maung Ing, Myat Rodgers suddenly appeared, as though waiting for them. He said little, but his rich clothes had lost their luster and he looked thinner. Each time he added some bananas, mangoes, or peanuts to the food to include his father, then disappeared as quickly as he came.

"That boy needs a family," Maung Ing had growled.

At the end of March, they were awakened early one morning by a *boom!* from the signal cannon on the river—followed by a second *boom!* The little household gathered on the porch of the mission house: What did it mean?

"General Bandula has won a victory, that's what it means," said Koo-Chill. He hurried off to the market as quickly as he could to hear the local gossip. Rumors were flying, but no one knew the facts.

Even the two signal guns did not change the prisoners' situation. The guards at the Death Prison took the daily food rations with a grunt and slammed the gates closed again. Len-Lay wondered if they even gave the food to the prisoners, or were letting them starve—but she didn't speak her worry aloud.

The mild, seventy-degree temperatures of Burma's "winter" gradually began to grow warmer and more humid. Then the signal cannon boomed again—once. This time the report that spread like wildfire through Ava was not rumor, but fact: The English had killed General Bandula in battle.

The people of Ava went into complete panic. Some families packed their belongings into ox carts and left the city. The Princess of Sarawaddy sent an urgent message for Mrs. Judson, who hurried to the palace with baby Maria and the two girls. Several other wives of court officials and the royal family were there.

What should they do, the women asked Mrs. Judson. Should they stay and face the English Redcoats bravely? Should they flee the city? Would the English soldiers kill them—or make them slaves . . . or worse?

"No, no," Mrs. Judson assured them. "The English do not kill civilians—especially women. In fact, they do not want Burma. If the Burmese army will stop fighting, they will make a treaty and leave."

The women looked at one another in amazement. They did not know whether to believe this foreign woman or not.

Six weeks had passed since Ann Judson had been allowed to see her husband, but she could not stop trying. Once more she trekked to the governor's house—and this time came home triumphant. He had finally given her permission to visit the prison!

Mrs. Judson left baby Maria at home with Ma-Noo and the girls and went to the prison, escorted by Maung Ing. But when she returned, Len-Lay saw that she had been crying.

"Mama Ann," she said, "did they turn you away?"

Mrs. Judson sank into the rocking chair and pulled the girls close. "No. They let Adoniram come to the door of the prison house. But . . . he now has *five* fetters on his legs; he can barely walk. And the filth! It is . . . unspeakably *horrible*." She dissolved in tears as the girls tried to comfort her.

A week later—May 2, 1825—Mrs. Judson went alone to try again to see her husband. Even with the governor's permission, it often took a long time to persuade the Spotted Faces to bring Mr. Judson out of the prison house. But taking food for the prisoners at least got her inside the gate.

Today she was gone an unusually long time, and Maung Ing had started to worry, when she came back smiling. "The strangest thing happened," Mrs. Judson said, mopping her damp face and sinking into the rocking chair. "The Spotted Faces let me speak to Adoniram, but then a servant came and said the governor wanted to see me right away. At first I was worried—but all he wanted to ask me about was his European watch, which wasn't keeping the right time! He served tea and we chatted for the longest time. But maybe it's a good sign; he was so friendly again."

Len-Lay brought baby Maria to nurse, and the girls settled down at Mrs. Judson's feet to do their reading lesson. Ma-Noo, Maung Ing, and Koo-Chill were arguing quietly about what to plant in the vegetable garden, when they heard a familiar voice outside, calling urgently.

"Maung Ing! Len-Lay! Mah-Lo! Come quickly!"

Len-Lay looked up, startled. "Why, that's Myat," she said.

The girls and Maung Ing rushed quickly out onto the porch, followed by Koo-Chill and Mrs. Judson. Myat Rodgers was holding on to the yard gate, trying to catch his breath.

"What is it, young son?" asked Maung Ing, hurrying to open the gate.

Myat kept his grip on the gate. "They're gone! They're all gone!" he gasped.

"Who's gone?" Maung Ing demanded.

"The prisoners! All the foreign prisoners have been taken away!"

"That's impossible," said Mrs. Judson. "I saw my husband just this morning."

"But I was just there!" insisted Myat. "I tell you, they are gone, and the Spotted Faces with them!"

"Where? Where have they gone?" said Maung Ing.

"I—I don't know," Myat said. "I asked everyone, but no one would tell me. They have just . . . disappeared!"

Chapter 10

The Trail to Oung-Pen-La

LEAVING BABY MARIA with Ma-Noo, Mrs. Judson, followed by Myat and the rest of the mission household, half-ran the two miles to the Death Prison to see for herself. "Open up! Open up!" she cried, banging on the outer gate.

The prison seemed strangely quiet. But after a long while, a Spotted Face opened the gate a few inches.

"I want to see my husband," Mrs. Judson demanded.

"Go away," sneered the Spotted Face. "He isn't here."

"Where? Where has he been taken?" she cried, but the gate slammed shut.

Frantic, Mrs. Judson looked wildly up and down

the dirt streets that surrounded the prison. Maung Ing stepped up to her and took her by the shoulders. "Mrs. *Yoodthan*, stop! Stop for a moment. We must think what to do."

Maung Ing's firm grip had a calming effect on Mrs. Judson. "Yes . . . yes, you are right. We must think."

Maung Ing lifted his face to the sky. "Our Father in heaven, hallowed be Your name . . ."

Mrs. Judson knelt in the dust and joined in the Lord's Prayer. Len-Lay, too, dropped to her knees and pulled Mah-Lo down beside her. Myat stood beside Koo-Chill and stared.

". . . Deliver us from the evil one. For Yours is the kingdom and the power and the glory forever. Amen." The little group got up from their knees.

"I must go back to the governor," Mrs. Judson said.

"Good idea," said Maung Ing. "Take Mah-Lo with you. The rest of us will scatter about the streets to see if we can learn anything."

As Mrs. Judson and Mah-Lo headed toward the governor's house, Maung Ing sent Koo-Chill and Len-Lay toward the marketplace and Myat toward the river, while he hurried off in another direction.

Following Koo-Chill's example, Len-Lay asked everyone she met, "Have you seen the foreign prisoners? Do you know where they've been taken?" One after another people just shook their heads or looked away as if they hadn't been asked. Len-Lay tried not to lose the Bengali cook as they worked their way up and down the market. Now and then she caught his eye, but he just shook his head: no luck.

Then she saw Koo-Chill talking to an old woman, who kept pointing in a certain direction. The old woman slipped into the crowd as Len-Lay grabbed Koo-Chill's arm.

"What did she say?" she asked anxiously.

Koo-Chill put a finger to his lips, took Len-Lay's hand and hurried toward the mission house. Mrs. Judson and Mah-Lo were already there talking to Ma-Noo; Maung Ing arrived shortly. Everyone started to talk at once, but Maung Ing said, "Hush! Hush! Listen to Mrs. *Yoodthan.*"

Mrs. Judson's face was tense with worry. "The governor found out just this morning that the new general—the one who replaced General Bandula; his name is Pakun Wan—ordered the prisoners to be taken someplace else. That's why he sent an urgent message for me to come to his house—to spare me, I suppose."

"Or keep you from making a scene," Koo-Chill muttered.

"One thing I know: they are still alive!" Maung Ing announced. "I went to the place where prisoners are executed; it was empty, and the blood was old."

Mrs. Judson's eyes brimmed with tears. "Thank God!" she exclaimed, sinking into the rocking chair.

Len-Lay tugged on Koo-Chill's arm. "What did that old woman say?"

All eyes turned on the Bengali cook.

"We were asking everyone we met if they'd seen

115

the foreign prisoners. An old woman whispered to me, 'Amarapura—look in Amarapura!' and she pointed north."

"The old royal city!" cried Maung Ing. "We must go there at once!"

"No . . . wait," said Mrs. Judson, wiping her tears. "We can't all go. Maung Ing—you must stay here with Ma-Noo and take care of the mission house. The girls will go with me; I need them to help with baby Maria. Koo-Chill will go with us."

Maung Ing started to protest as everyone began talking at once. Then, out on the porch, they heard a familiar voice calling, "Hello? Hello? Anybody home?"

Maung Ing and the girls rushed outside. There, perched on the porch railing, was Mr. Beg Pardon. He cocked his head at them and said, "Hello!"

Maung Ing's face revealed a mixture of amazement and delight. The girls grinned from ear to ear as he carefully scooped up the bright green parrot and put him back in his wicker cage.

Mrs. Judson, standing at the door, smiled as new tears slid down her face. "Welcome home, Mr. Beg Pardon. Maybe God sent you back . . . as a sign of hope!"

Len-Lay woke up, stiff and sore, and looked around. She had fallen asleep on the deck of the little covered boat Koo-Chill had found yesterday. Koo-Chill was sitting in the bow, a big arm around Mah-Lo who sat in his lap. Nearby Mrs. Judson was nursing a restless Maria.

So much had happened in the last twenty-four hours! Mrs. Judson had packed two trunks with clothes, sleeping mats, a few pots for cooking, and several pretty trinkets for bribes. Then Koo-Chill went off, looking for a boat that would take them the four miles up the Irrawaddy River to Amarapura, which had been the royal city when King Bagyidaw's father had been king.

But no one had seen Myat Rodgers since they'd all scattered in different directions from the Death Prison. Len-Lay worried about him. Even though he was fourteen now and almost a man—it was over a year since they'd first met—he seemed lost with no family and nowhere to turn.

They had spent one last night in the mission house, then got up early to follow the trail of the prisoners. "I will see if I can find Myat," Maung Ing assured Len-Lay as she climbed into the boat. Then he stood on the bank of the river, Mr. Beg Pardon on his shoulder, waving goodbye in the early morning light.

Now the sun was high overhead. Len-Lay's head ached and her mouth was dry. She crawled farther under the thatch shelter and closed her eyes again.

When she awoke a second time, the boatman was poling the boat into the landing at Amarapura. She wondered why she felt so tired. She helped Koo-Chill and Mah-Lo unload the baggage, then sank onto a trunk while the Bengali cook went off looking for a cart.

Mrs. Judson paced up and down the landing with baby Maria in her arms while they waited. At last, Koo-Chill appeared with a driver and a creaking, solid-wheel cart, pulled by a scrawny ox. "Try the courthouse," Mrs. Judson said as they piled in. It was another two miles across Amarapura to the courthouse, and the two-wheeled cart pitched and groaned the whole way.

Koo-Chill found water while Mrs. Judson went inside to talk to the local magistrate. Len-Lay drank the cool water gratefully, but shook her head when Koo-Chill offered her a smoked fish. She wasn't hungry.

Finally, Mrs. Judson came out. "The prisoners have been taken to the village of Oung-Pen-La," she said wearily. "Another four miles north."

The driver didn't want to go, and Koo-Chill haggled with him for half an hour in the hot sun before he finally accepted a hefty bribe of silver ticals. By now both baby Maria and Mah-Lo were crying with the heat and exhaustion.

The ox cart jostled mile after mile over the rutted trail toward Oung-Pen-La, and gritty dust stirred up by the oxen's hooves settled in everyone's eyes and ears and mouth. The sun blazed hot and unrelenting, and Len-Lay's headache worsened.

The sun had dropped behind the treetops when the ox cart creaked through the little village of Oung-Pen-La. Mrs. Judson urged the driver on a little way beyond the village until they arrived at the "prison": a run-down bamboo shack, barely more than a platform four feet off the ground, with a thatch roof that was falling in. Surrounding the shack was a stockade fence—or what was left of it.

Len-Lay could see the prisoners lying on the platform while several villagers tried to repair the roof overhead. Hastily, Koo-Chill helped Mrs. Judson out of the cart, unloaded the trunks, and paid off the surly driver.

There were only three jailers and they were *not* Spotted Faces. The head jailer shrugged when Ann Judson asked to speak to the prisoners. Climbing the little steps leading to the platform, the travelers saw that the prisoners were chained together, two by two. Their clothes were mere rags hanging on their bony bodies; their hair was matted and greasy. But worst of all, their feet were covered with raw, bloody blisters from the painful two-day march from Ava.

"Adoniram," said Mrs. Judson softly.

Mr. Judson—barely recognizable—half-opened his eyes.

"Oh, Ann," he groaned. "Why did you come? I hoped you would not follow us." Then he sank back into a stupor.

In spite of their terrible condition, Len-Lay was glad to see Mr. Judson, Henry Gouger, Dr. Price, and even Mr. Rodgers alive—and out of the awful Death Prison. Koo-Chill gave them each some water, then the little group gathered under a tree to think about what *they* were going to do for food and shelter.

The head jailer, somewhat flustered by the arrival of both the prisoners and their visitors—the prison at Oung-Pen-La had obviously been empty for years—took pity on Mrs. Judson and her homeless family and invited them to stay in his own home overnight. The bamboo-and-thatch house had two rooms; the jailer's family lived in one, the other was used to store grain. Koo-Chill and Mrs. Judson spread out the sleeping mats among the piles of grain.

"Mama Ann," Len-Lay whispered as Mrs. Judson kissed her good night. "I don't feel good."

"I know, I know," her foster mother whispered back. "It's been a miserable day. You will probably feel better after a good sleep."

But Len-Lay did not have a good sleep. The headache pounded behind her eyes; all night long she heard what sounded like flying insects droning in her ears. She felt hot and restless. Sometimes she thought she was still being tossed around in the uncomfortable ox cart.

Toward morning she fell into a troubled sleep; she dreamed she was running and running, trying to find her father, Maung Shway-Bay . . . then she was looking for Myat Rodgers . . . and calling and calling for Mr. Beg Pardon.

"She has a fever," she heard someone say. It was Koo-Chill's voice.

"Look, Mama Ann," said a girl's voice. "She has funny spots on her face."

A woman's voice. "Oh, Koo-Chill, do you think—"

"I don't know." Koo-Chill said. "But it might be."

"O God in heaven. What are we going to do?"

"What is it, Mama Ann? What's the matter with Len-Lay?"

There was silence. Len-Lay thought maybe she was still dreaming. Her head hurt and she felt so hot. Then she heard Mrs. Judson's voice again.

"She has smallpox."

Chapter 11

The Tiger

WHEN DR. PRICE HEARD Mrs. Judson describe Len-Lay's symptoms—high fever, headache, vomiting, small red spots spreading from her face to her back and arms—he confirmed the diagnosis.

After a few days the fever went down, but soon the little red spots had turned into watery blisters all over Len-Lay's body. She lay in the grain room of the jailer's house, too sick and too tired to care much about what was happening outside.

Mrs. Judson was spooning some broth into Len-Lay's mouth when Koo-Chill came back after visiting the prisoners. "Henry Gouger's servant showed up today with a sack of rice and some salt fish that he wants all of us to share," he reported. "That takes care of the food problem for the moment."

Mrs. Judson nodded, but her thoughts were elsewhere. "I'm worried about Abby and baby Maria. I was vaccinated against smallpox in America—but of course the children are not. They are sure to come down with the disease, too."

"Oh, that's the other thing," Koo-Chill said, taking the bowl of broth from Mrs. Judson. "Dr. Price wants to talk to you at the prison. Don't worry. I had the smallpox when I was a boy." Koo-Chill waved her away and spooned the last of the broth down Len-Lay's throat.

When Mrs. Judson returned from the prison, her eyes revealed that she was a little frightened, but she began digging with determination in one of the trunks. "Dr. Price said I should vaccinate the other children right away, before Mary becomes too infectious. Koo-Chill, please find Abby—she's playing with the baby somewhere. Now . . . where are those candles we packed?"

Koo-Chill brought Mah-Lo and baby Maria into the grain room, Mrs. Judson had lit a candle from the jailer's wife's cooking fire and was

123

sterilizing one of her sewing needles in the flame. "Mary and Abby, listen carefully," she said gently. "I'm going to prick one of Mary's blisters with this needle; then I'm going to prick your arm, Abby. Then I'm going to do the same thing to Maria. You must hold very still so I don't hurt you."

The jailer's wife, watching from the doorway, was very curious. When Mrs. Judson explained what she was doing, the woman disappeared, but in a few minutes was back with her four naked children. "Please give them the *small* smallpox," she said. Later she told Koo-Chill, "If the American woman will prick her own children with the smallpox, then it must be a good thing."

Len-Lay's blisters, however, soon filled with pus and the high fever returned. Nights merged with days as low, urgent voices moved in and out of her consciousness. Her body felt on fire; she wanted to tear off her skin. But she couldn't move her hands! She thrashed and pulled and cried out, then fell into an exhausted sleep.

On the twelfth day after leaving Ava, Len-Lay opened her eyes, staring at the unfamiliar room. Where was she? Where was Ma-Noo and Maung Ing and Mr. Beg Pardon? Then slowly she remembered: She was in the jailer's house in Oung-Pen-La and she'd been very, very sick.

She tried to get up, but her hands were tied to the floor with soft rags. "Mama Ann!" she cried out, frightened.

Mrs. Judson was immediately at her side, untying the rags. "Hush, dear Mary," she soothed. "We had to tie your hands to keep you from scratching the pox and spreading the infection. There—you are free." Her foster mother smiled. "Praise God. The fever has broken. You are going to get well."

But Len-Lay had to stay inside the grain room for another week while the blisters broke and formed scabs. Mah-Lo, meanwhile, popped in and out with all the latest news.

"The jailers rebuilt the stockade around the prison and the prisoners have to sleep with their feet locked in the stocks. . . . But we can visit any time we want . . . and the jailer lets the prisoners walk around inside the stockade during the day . . . and there are no *rats* . . . and the jailer's wife washed their clothes and Mama Ann made all the prisoners take a bath."

Here Mah-Lo broke into peals of laughter. "She made all the children go outside the stockade, but some of the boys climbed the trees to watch. They wanted to know what color skin the prisoners had underneath all that dirt!" And then the younger girl flew off to play with the jailer's children.

When Mrs. Judson finally allowed Len-Lay to go with her to the prison to visit, all the prisoners were looking much better than the last time she'd seen them. Their feet had healed and they wore only one pair of chains on their wrists and ankles. Mr. Judson and the others greeted her warmly, though they, too, were just regaining some of their strength from the eleven bitter months in the Death Prison.

"Ann, have you heard anyone say why we have

been brought here?" Mr. Judson asked his wife anxiously.

She shook her head. "All I know is that the new general, Pakun-Wun, gave the orders. We are renting a room from the jailer's family, and all he says is 'the Tiger' sent you here."

"When the Spotted Faces left us here, they said we were going to be burned alive," Dr. Price added. "But I don't think they would repair the roof of this pitiful pen if they were going to kill us."

"Don't be too sure," Mr. Rodgers spoke up. Len-Lay was startled. It was the first time she'd heard him join the conversation. "General Pakun-Wun— the pompous pig calls himself the 'Tiger'—was born here in Oung-Pen-La. My guess is that he plans to make some nasty example of us when he defeats the English."

As they were about to leave, Len-Lay heard Mr. Judson say to his wife, "Is there any news about my pillow?"

Ann stared at him. "No one was thinking about the pillow, Adoniram! We were afraid for your very life!"

He sighed. "The Spotted Faces drove us out of the Death Prison so fast, no one had time to take anything. I—I am afraid it is lost forever . . ." He stared into the distance with deep, sad eyes. "Oh, Ann. So many years of work—gone. I have failed in every way. Burma is lost, lost."

Len-Lay had forgotten about the ugly, brown pillow with the mysterious package inside. *What was*

Papa 'Don talking about?

The vaccination of Mah-Lo and the jailer's children was a great success: They all developed smallpox, but so mildly it hardly interrupted their play. But poor baby Maria became very sick; like Len-Lay, the ugly blisters covered her from head to toe, and she fretted and cried for days.

But the villagers of Oung-Pen-La had heard about the vaccinations. When they saw the jailer's children escaping the terrible sickness, many of them brought their children to Mrs. Judson to be vaccinated, too. However, the stress of taking care of two sick children in a row, bartering with the villagers for food, vaccinating their children, and feeding and encouraging the prisoners began to take its toll on her. She was tired and began losing weight.

Still, when baby Maria was almost recovered from the smallpox, Mrs. Judson left the two older children with Koo-Chill and hired a cart from the village to take her to Amarapura for supplies and medicine. She was gone several days, and Koo-Chill, a deep frown creased across his broad face, began watching the road.

Finally the cart appeared. Even before it drew close, the girls could hear six-month-old Maria wailing. Koo-Chill and the girls ran to the cart. Mrs. Judson lay crumpled on the bottom of the cart with baby Maria crying against her chest.

"Dysentery, I think," mumbled the driver, jerking his head at Mrs. Judson. Len-Lay scooped up the baby while Koo-Chill gently picked up Mrs. Judson in his strong arms and carried her into the grain room of the jailer's house and laid her on her mat.

Mrs. Judson was so ill she could do nothing for herself, much less take care of the baby. Maria was already crying constantly with hunger. Koo-Chill, reluctant to leave Mrs. Judson's side except to make food for the family and the prisoners, said urgently, "Len-Lay, the baby must have mother's milk to live. Tell the jailer he must find a Burmese woman to nurse her!"

Feeling helpless, Len-Lay picked up the crying baby, so thin her little arms and legs looked like sticks, and hurried in search of the jailer. How could she make him pay attention to her? She was just a girl, practically a stranger. If only Mama Ann could tell her what to do!

Len-Lay found the jailer at the prison repairing the stocks that held the prisoners' feet each night. Hearing Maria's cries, Mr. Judson hurried to Len-Lay's side as fast as his chains would allow and took the wailing infant into his own arms. Without time to think, Len-Lay spoke directly to the jailer.

"O paddy father," she said, bowing respectfully, "you know the wife of the American missionary is very sick; she has no milk for her baby. We must find a woman to nurse her or the child will die."

The jailer scowled. "That is not my concern," he said gruffly. "First, I am sent prisoners with no warning. My rice field suffers with neglect. Then the prisoner's family moves in with me! Now everyone is sick. No! No! No! I will not—"

"O generous paddy father," Mr. Judson broke in, trying to speak calmly over Maria's screams. "I am very grateful for all you have done for me and my family. I would not ask you to find a nurse for my child. Only . . . let me go to the village and I will find a kind woman to take pity on us."

"Impossible!" snapped the jailer.

Mama Ann never accepted *impossible* as an answer, Len-Lay thought. "We will give you presents," she spoke up quickly. "A length of silk for your wife . . . and silver ticals for you." Even as she spoke, Len-Lay gulped. How dare she offer presents to the jailer—things that did not even belong to her! But out of the corner of her eye, she saw Mr. Judson give a faint smile.

And so it was decided: Mr. Judson could take baby Maria into the village three times a day—his wrists and ankles safely chained, of course—seeking a Burmese woman to nurse the child. Len-Lay or Mah-Lo would bring the baby to the prison, then go with him into the village. But it was Mr. Judson himself, in his chains, begging milk for his starving child, who drew sympathy from the village women.

In this way little Maria survived, and gradually Mrs. Judson began to recover. News of the war was sparse, but now and then reports trickled in: The English had captured the city of Prome, but had come no farther . . . General Pakun-Wun was going city to city, village to village, raising a new army to fight the English . . . The new troops were untrained, but at least they were a large number.

Rumors were also whispered about the fate of the prisoners. The name of the village, Oung-Pen-La, meant "Field of Victory." The prisoners (according to the rumors) were going to be buried alive in front of the Burmese troops as they marched off to fight the English. General Pakun-Wun was supposedly saying, "Planting the foreign prisoners in the Field of Victory could only result in a harvest of victory against the foreign invaders!"

Then one night, Len-Lay awoke to loud roars coming from the direction of the village. "Mama Ann!" she screamed. "A tiger has come out of the jungle!"

But then they heard Koo-Chill's voice say, "What is this madness? Come and see!"

Len-Lay and Mah-Lo ran out onto the porch; Mrs. Judson, the jailer, and his family joined them. There, stopping right in front of the house, was a wooden cage on wheels pulled by six men, accompanied by four soldiers. Inside the cage, pacing back and forth in the small space, was a tiger. The beast's ribs stuck out and it roared with hunger again and again.

"Where is the head jailer?" yelled one of the soldiers, trying to be heard over the tiger's roars.

"Right here!" yelled back the jailer, wearing only a loincloth and mad as a bull at being awakened in the middle of the night. "What is the meaning of this?"

"Open up the stockade!" the soldier demanded. "We have another prisoner for you!"

"What? You must be crazy! I'm not going to put a starving tiger in *my* prison!"

The soldier glared at the jailer. "Open the stockade, you wretch. By order of General Pakun-Wun!"

Chapter 12

The Open Cage

THE NEXT MORNING Len-Lay and Mah-Lo walked nervously up to the prison gate with food for the prisoners. There it was inside the stockade: the tiger, pacing back and forth in its cage. Now and then the beast let out an unhappy roar.

The prisoners weren't too happy, either. "How do you like our new companion, eh, Mary and Abby?" said Mr. Judson with a tired smile, taking the food from the girls. He obviously hadn't slept much the night before.

Henry Gouger gave a short laugh. "General Pakun-Wun has a strange sense of humor."

"Humor, nothing!" barked Mr. Rodgers angrily. "He probably means to feed *us* to the tiger when he gets around to it."

"Be quiet, Rodgers," said Dr. Price. "There's no need to frighten these young ladies." He turned a critical eye on Len-Lay. "The scars from the pox aren't too bad, Mary Hasseltine . . . By the way, have you heard any news of my wife, Ma-Noo?"

Len-Lay shook her head, keeping her eyes on the tiger. The tiger glared back, baring his teeth. She was frightened by it, but she also felt sorry for it. "Is the jailer going to feed it?" she asked timidly.

"No, I am not!" an angry voice boomed behind her. It was the head jailer, who had just arrived to inspect his new "prisoner" by daylight. "I don't have any orders to feed this . . . this miserable creature." The jailer stomped around, waving his hands and glaring at everybody. "We are a poor village! Does the general think we have extra goats running around just begging lord tiger to eat them?" And with that he went stomping out of the stockade again.

"I don't think goats are what Pakun-Wun has in mind," muttered Mr. Rodgers again.

The girls agreed not to tell Mrs. Judson what Mr. Rodgers had said. But at night, when they heard the tiger roaring again and again with hunger, they lay on their mats with thumping hearts. Why had the tiger come? What if Mr. Rodgers was right? What if General Pakun-Wun ordered the prisoners to be thrown inside that terrible cage?

One night as they got ready for bed, with the tiger roaring almost nonstop in the background, Mrs. Judson pulled the girls close and said, "I want to tell you a story. It's a true story about a man named Daniel who lived a long time ago. Daniel had been captured in a war and taken to a strange land as a slave. The king of that country liked Daniel, however, and gave him an important position in the king's court—"

"Like Mr. Rodgers had?" Mah-Lo interrupted.

"Yes, something like that. Except Daniel loved the true God in heaven. And every day he prayed to God—even though it was against the law of that land to pray to anyone except the king."

Len-Lay noticed that Koo-Chill was sitting in the doorway of the grain room, listening to the story, too.

"One day Daniel's enemies told the king that Daniel prayed every day to the God in heaven. This made the king sad, because he had made a law that said anyone caught praying to another God would get thrown into a den of lions!"

Mah-Lo sucked in her breath.

"But . . . it was the law, so the king's men threw Daniel into the lions' den."

Len-Lay started to shiver. Now she knew Mrs. Judson was also wondering if the prisoners were going to be fed to the hungry tiger. But why was she telling this terrible story?

"The next day the king went to the lions' den, certain he would find Daniel's body torn to pieces. But there was Daniel sitting in the lions' den without a scratch!"

"Impossible!" muttered Koo-Chill from the doorway. Mrs. Judson pretended to ignore him.

"The king was so excited he ordered his men to take Daniel out of the den. Daniel told him, 'I prayed

to my God and asked Him to shut the mouths of the lions, and as you see, they did not hurt me!'"

Mrs. Judson's voice suddenly softened. "So, dear Mary and Abby, let's pray that God will shut the mouth of this tiger—and shut the mouth of General Tiger, as well!"

Two weeks had passed since the tiger arrived. Then one morning Len-Lay woke up feeling strange; something was different. Then she realized what it was: the silence.

The tiger was no longer roaring from the prison stockade.

"Mama Ann!" she cried out. A rush of fear choked off her words. *What if General Pakun-Wun had ordered—?*

But Mrs. Judson was already scrambling down from the porch of the jailer's house with baby Maria and running to the prison. Len-Lay, Mah-Lo, and Koo-Chill followed fast on her heels.

As they ran up the road, the prison gate swung open and the jailer marched out. "Out of the way!" he yelled. "Get back, get back!"

Behind him several villagers backed out of the gate, dragging the dead body of the tiger. By now it was just skin and bones.

"The poor thing," murmured Mrs. Judson. "It starved to death."

Koo-Chill looked relieved and irritated at the same time. "Don't pity the beast. *You* asked your God to shut the tiger's mouth, didn't you?" And he turned around and marched back to the jailer's house.

Within a few days, one of Gouger's servants arrived at the prison with news, and it became clear why the jailer had never received any further orders. General Pakun-Wun was dead!

"What?" cried Mr. Rodgers as the two families from the jailer's house gathered with the prisoners in the stockade. "Was he killed in a battle with the English?"

Gouger's servant shook his head, eyes dancing. "No, no. The Tiger asked King Bagyidaw for permission to command the troop of royal princes; the king said no, because Pakun-Wun was not royalty himself. Then Pakun-Wun asked for the king's personal bodyguard to go with him to the war; the king became suspicious. The general next asked the king to go to the Mengoon Pagoda—outside of Ava—to pray for the battle's success."

"Sounds like a plot to take away the king's guard and then take away the king's throne!" grinned Henry Gouger.

The servant nodded vigorously. "Exactly what King Bagyidaw thought! The king ordered Pakun-Wun to be dragged from the Golden Presence. He was beaten and kicked all the way to the place of execution—I saw him myself—where the white elephants trampled him to death."

For a few moments everyone was silent. Len-Lay tried not to think about the elephants . . . on the other hand, she felt enormously relieved. Suddenly everyone began talking at once and Henry Gouger attempted a little dance, whooping and hollering as

137

he hopped and skipped in his chains.

"I don't think we have to fear any death threats now," the young Englishman finally said. "It's the English army's turn to move; we are valuable as hostages now."

Mah-Lo tugged on Koo-Chill's sleeve. "I think God shut the other Tiger's mouth, too."

"Humph!" said the big Bengali cook.

The two sisters grinned at each other. That was Len-Lay's thought, exactly.

The jailer wanted to remove the empty tiger cage, but Mr. Judson asked for permission to clean it and use it as his own private "cell." Shrugging, the jailer agreed, locking Mr. Judson inside each evening and opening the cage door each morning so he could walk about the stockade with the others.

With immediate death no longer hanging over the prisoners' heads, Mr. Judson seemed to find the energy to do more thinking. He even asked for pen and paper so he could do some writing in the tiger cage.

Mrs. Judson often sat with him for a short while each day, comforting the fretful Maria. Len-Lay saw Mr. Judson often looking at his wife and child with worried eyes; both were thin and frail. The long months of prison life, sickness, and poor food was wearing them out.

One day Len-Lay was playing with baby Maria

nearby as her foster parents talked in the tiger cage. "I have not been much of a husband to you, nor a very good father to our children," Mr. Judson said forlornly to his wife.

"Hush, hush," Mrs. Judson said. "Is it your fault? You have suffered so much."

Mr. Judson nodded. "I know. But I also wanted to give up; I did not have patience to stand the trial the Lord has asked of me." He held up his hand before his wife could interrupt. "I never told you that I was tempted to throw myself into the river and end it all—that day we were taken out of the Death Prison and marched to Oung-Pen-La."

There was silence in the tiger cage for a few moments, then Mr. Judson spoke again.

"I complained bitterly to God about losing the pillow with the book inside—"

Len-Lay's ears perked up. *Book? What book?*

"—and my faith has wavered. Does He know and care that we sit here like chained dogs? Or has He forsaken us completely? We came to Burma to be missionaries. But what have we accomplished in the last sixteen months? Nothing!"

"Oh, Adoniram!"

"But I have been thinking," the American missionary went on. "Jesus said a grain of wheat must fall into the ground and die before it can bear any fruit."

"But you have borne fruit!" cried Mrs. Judson. "Look at Maung Ing, and Maung Shway-Bay, and the other Burmese Christians! We—we don't know

139

what happened to the little Rangoon church, but surely some have survived the war. Each one is a seed, planted in Burma."

Mr. Judson nodded. "You are right. That is what I've been thinking. It's just that . . . I didn't realize how hard it would be to be that grain of wheat and die."

Henry Gouger was right. The English were getting closer to Ava and the Burmese were beginning to realize they would have to make peace sometime. But no one in the Burmese royal court could speak English, and no one in the English camp could speak Burmese. Suddenly the prisoners wasting away at Oung-Pen-La were remembered. They could speak both English and Burmese!

In August, a band of flustered officials showed up at the prison one day and carted all the prisoners off to Amarapura. When they returned to the prison later that night, Mr. Judson told Ann and the girls that each one had been put in a separate room, then asked to translate an English document one at a time. The results were then compared to see if the English-speaking prisoners could be trusted to translate truthfully.

Still, more than two months dragged by as rumors of peace treaties being offered and rejected floated through Oung-Pen-La. Then on November 4, 1825, a soldier dismounted from his horse in front of the prison. He had the tip of an elephant tusk slung under his arm, decorated with blood-red tassels—it was the king's own message case—from which he withdrew a palm leaf.

It was an order for Adoniram Judson's release. He was to go at once to the Golden Presence. The king needed an interpreter to discuss terms for ending the war.

Len-Lay and Mah-Lo, who had come running with Ann Judson and Koo-Chill, could hardly believe their ears. They were going home to Ava!

Mr. Rodgers spoke up. "What about me? I have served the king faithfully for forty years! I can be his interpreter."

The soldier scowled. "You are English, old man!" he shouted. "The king needs an interpreter who is neither English nor Burmese. He wants the American and no other. Now, jailer, strike off those chains!"

Chapter 13

Saved From the Trash Heap

I T WAS AN EMOTIONAL PARTING the next morning. Mr. Judson was eager to get his wife and children back to Ava where they could have a decent roof over their heads and adequate food. But it was hard to leave his fellow prisoners behind, still in chains.

Mr. Rodgers swallowed his pride and said, "You're a decent man, Judson. Put in a good word for us with the king, will you?"

Sitting in the rented cart, crowded with their trunks and sleeping mats, Len-Lay wondered if Mr. Rodgers remembered the day he had refused to speak to the king on the Judsons' behalf.

"Of course!" Mr. Judson said. "I will make sure the release of all foreign prisoners is part of any peace treaty."

"We'll miss your wife more than we'll miss you!" Dr. Price said, trying to make a joke. "Mrs. Judson, you have been an angel sent from God, a drink of cool water to our parched souls . . ." His voice wavered, and the doctor turned away abruptly, unable to stop the tears.

"Don't worry about us," said Henry Gouger cheerfully. "But I want you to know, Adoniram, it is you who gave us spiritual strength to endure these long terrible months in prison."

"Oh, Henry. If you only knew how many times my faith stumbled—"

"So you are human! Your faith may have stumbled, but it did not die. And . . ." Here Henry Gouger's voice began to tremble. ". . . as long as you held on, we were able to hang on, too."

The soldier was getting impatient to leave. With a gift of silver ticals, Mrs. Judson persuaded the jailer's wife to cook food for the other prisoners, supplemented by what Gouger's servant could bring from Ava once a week, until the prisoners were released.

"Goodbye! Goodbye!" called the girls, as the ox cart began to lurch down the rutted road. Then, with Koo-Chill and Mr. Judson walking alongside the cart and the soldier bringing up the rear, the little band turned their faces toward Amarapura, then Ava—and home.

❖ ❖ ❖

In Amarapura, the soldier separated Mr. Judson from his family and took him first to the courthouse, then on to Ava directly to the king's palace. Koo-Chill again found a boat to take the rest of the family down the Irrawaddy River to Ava.

Has it only been six months since we left Ava looking for the prisoners? Len-Lay thought as the boatman put up his sail. It seemed like years ago.

The sun had hidden behind the trees to the west but it was still light when Mrs. Judson, the girls, and Koo-Chill unloaded the boat and scrambled up the bank to the mission house. Len-Lay and Mah-Lo ran ahead. There was the fence around the yard . . . the vegetable garden and the acacia tree . . . and Mr. Beg Pardon hanging in his wicker cage from the porch roof!

"Maung Ing! Ma-Noo!" they shouted. "We're home! We're home!"

"Hello! Hello!" squawked Mr. Beg Pardon.

Maung Ing flung open the door; his mouth dropped open and his eyes widened. "Wha—? Oh, praise the Lord in heaven! You've come back!"

The Burmese man scurried down the porch steps, bowing and grinning and taking bags and bowing again. Ma-Noo appeared at the door, smiling happily. Len-Lay hurried up onto the porch to let the blind woman "see" they were really home by touching her. That's when the girl realized someone else was standing behind Ma-Noo.

144

It was Myat Rodgers.

"Myat! I'm so glad you're all right—!"

But at that moment, Mrs. Judson and baby Maria and Mah-Lo all crowded onto the porch, followed shortly by Maung Ing and Koo-Chill with the trunks and bags. Inside everyone was asking questions at once until suddenly Ma-Noo clapped her hands.

"Sit down! Sit down!" she ordered. "Let's have tea. *Then* we will talk."

Len-Lay wanted to ask Myat what he was doing at the mission house. But Koo-Chill put her to work helping Ma-Noo set tea and fruit and cold rice and smoked fish on the table. Koo-Chill insisted that Mrs. Judson eat something before trying to talk.

But finally the story all came out—about the prison in Oung-Pen-La and the smallpox and the starving tiger in the cage and finally the king's order to release Mr. Judson to act as translator between the English and the Burmese.

"What about my father?"

It was the first time Myat had spoken since they arrived. All eyes turned to the boy. He was fifteen now, and had grown taller. Len-Lay thought he was . . . different, somehow.

"Your father is alive and . . . doing well," said Mrs. Judson carefully. Though the conditions at Oung-Pen-La had been better than in the Death Prison, all the prisoners were thin and in poor health. "I'm sure he will be released soon. He will be so glad to know that you are all right."

Maung Ing grinned from ear to ear and clapped a

hand on Myat's shoulder. "We, too, have a story to tell! Myat, tell what happened that day the prisoners disappeared, after we all scattered around the city trying to find where they had been taken."

Myat looked embarrassed. But at Maung Ing's urging he started his story.

"I went to the river to see if my father and the other prisoners had been taken away by boat. But no one had seen them. Instead of coming back to the mission house to see if the rest of you had discovered anything, I wandered back to the Death Prison—the last place I'd seen my father. Maybe he'd left something behind, something I could remember him by."

Len-Lay smiled at Myat encouragingly.

"I banged on the gate, but the Spotted Faces wouldn't let me in. So I just wandered around the outside of the prison, not knowing what to do. In the back of the prison was a big trash heap. I was so crazy with grief, I started digging through all the garbage, trying to find something—anything—that belonged to my father. But I found nothing—"

The boy paused. "Go on! Go on!" Maung Ing urged.

"I found nothing—except an ugly old pillow. I recognized it as the one Len-Lay brought to the prison for Mr. Judson."

Mrs. Judson gasped. "Hush! Hush!" she said to baby Maria who had started to whimper.

"I was so angry I started tearing the pillow apart," Myat said, "and that's when I found *the Book*. Well, it didn't look like a book really. Just lots and lots of pages with writing on it. I stuffed the pages back in the pillow and ran home with it, thinking, 'Now I'll find the proof I need that Mr. Judson is a spy!'"

Len-Lay's eyes widened. Had Myat found something that would get Mr. Judson thrown back in prison? She looked anxiously at Mrs. Judson, but her foster mother was nursing Maria, a slight smile on her lips.

"The writing was Burmese," Myat went on, "so I began to read. But it was a story about a man named Jesus . . . and that's when I knew that Mr. Judson really was a religion teacher after all, and not a spy."

"A story?" Mah-Lo blurted.

"That's all that was in the pillow?" Len-Lay echoed. "A story?"

Mrs. Judson smiled. "Not just a story, Mary and Abby. It was the whole *New Testament*—the part of the Christian Bible that tells all about God's Son, Jesus. Adoniram had spent years translating it into the Burmese language. He finished just before we left Rangoon to come to Ava. I hid it in the pillow because I was afraid the magistrate would take it away and destroy it. But when the prisoners disappeared from the Death Prison . . ." Her voice dropped to a whisper. "We thought it was lost forever."

"No! No! It was found!" laughed Maung Ing. "But go on, Myat, go on!"

Now Myat was smiling, too. "I kept on reading and couldn't stop. This Jesus was unlike any man I've ever met! But I had so many questions—"

One day Myat came to the mission house asking for Maung Ing. "I have many questions about this

147

Jesus person," he'd said.

Overjoyed that the pillow and its precious contents had been found, Maung Ing was eager to talk with Myat about what he'd been reading. He invited Myat to stay with him and Ma-Noo at the mission house while they studied the Word of God together. And Ma-Noo was only too glad to have a young person to fuss over.

As they finished their story, Maung Ing went and stood behind Myat, putting his hands on the boy's shoulders. "You are looking at a new Christian disciple," he said proudly. "In Mr. Judson's absence, I prepared him for baptism and—"

"Dunked me in the Irrawaddy!" laughed Myat.

Everyone cheered and clapped.

"My heart is full of joy!" said Mrs. Judson, giving Myat a hug. "Myat, you are welcome to stay with us until your father is released from prison. But, now, it is very late. We must all go to bed. Maybe tomorrow Mr. Judson will come."

Tired from the long trip, the girls slept late. But finally, loud squawks from the porch awoke them.

"Hello! Hello! Beg your pardon! Who's coming? Awwk!"

Then they heard Mrs. Judson cry out, "It's Adoniram!"

The girls scrambled up from their sleeping mat and hurried into the main room of the bamboo house.

Mr. Judson had encircled his wife and baby in his arms. Then he greeted Ma-Noo and the beaming Maung Ing.

Through the front door Len-Lay could see two soldiers waiting out by the yard gate.

"I can't stay," Mr. Judson said quickly. "The king is sending me down the river—under guard—to meet with the English general and return with the terms of the peace treaty. It might mean going back and forth several times—maybe a few weeks, maybe a few months."

"Oh, Adoniram." The smile left Ann Judson's face.

"But once the peace treaty has been signed, the king has promised that I will be free to go—and the other prisoners as well," said Mr. Judson. He looked tired, but he smiled at the girls. "Now—I only have a few minutes to get a few things. Can you spare a sleeping mat and a blanket?"

"How about a pillow?" Myat spoke up as he placed the ugly prison pillow in Mr. Judson's arms.

No one spoke or moved. Mr. Judson stared at the pillow, astonished. Then, clasping the pillow to his chest, the missionary sank to his knees. "O God, my Father!" he whispered hoarsely. "You did not abandon me. You protected this work, so that Burma might have Your Word in their own language. Lord, I believe! Help my unbelief."

The soldiers began shouting from the gate. "Hurry, Mr. Yoodthan! We must catch the boat!"

"Hurry! Hurry!" squawked Mr. Beg Pardon.

There was a flurry of good-byes. A soft pillow was substituted for the hard, prison one, along with a blanket and sleeping mat. And then Mr. Judson headed for the river as everyone waved to him from the porch.

As the mission household came back inside, Koo-Chill cleared his throat loudly.

"Harumph!"

Everyone stopped and looked at the Bengali cook. He was holding the prison pillow.

"With your permission, Mrs. *Yoodthan*," he said, bowing respectfully, "I would—uh—also like to read

150

the writings inside the pillow. I like stories, and these must be very good stories indeed. Is the story of Daniel and the lions in this book?"

Mrs. Judson laughed. "No, that story is in the *Old Testament*, which hasn't been translated yet. But I would very much like you to read the stories about Jesus, Koo-Chill. Then, when we return to Rangoon, there is a missionary there who can print copies for us, so that many people in Burma can read God's Word."

Len-Lay and Mah-Lo looked at each other. Mrs. Judson had said, "When we return to Rangoon." That meant they would soon see their own father, Maung Shway-Bay! Then Len-Lay remembered: The last thing their father had said was, "Teach them to read so they can read Jesus' words on the paper you have written."

"Mama Ann," said Len-Lay, "could we start our school again while we're waiting for Papa 'Don? I want to be able to read the Bible, too."

Mah-Lo nodded eagerly.

"Watch out," said Myat, grinning at Koo-Chill. "Reading that book might change your life."

More About
Ann and Adoniram Judson

A DONIRAM JUDSON was born August 9, 1788, in Bradford, Massachusetts, the son of a Congregationalist minister. At the age of sixteen he entered Brown University, graduating after only three years. Questioning his faith, the young man set out to "see the world," but after the shocking death of a friend, returned home and entered Andover Seminary at age twenty where he made a "solemn dedication" of himself to God.

Young Judson soon determined to be the first American foreign missionary—a calling shared by his sweetheart Ann Hasseltine, who was only a year younger. In February 1812, Ann and Adoniram were married; two weeks later the newlyweds set sail for India, accompanied by another young couple.

But the British East India Company was hostile to the young missionaries and threatened to deport them. Uncertain where to establish a mission work, the Judsons finally arrived in Rangoon, Burma—a year and a half after leaving America.

Unlike India, which had a large European population because of the East India Company, only a handful of white foreigners lived in Burma. Though the majority of the Burmese people lived in poverty under the thumb of a cruel and unpredictable monarchy, there was no caste system (which in India strictly divided people according to class, race, and status). The language was difficult, and the Judsons spent twelve hours a day in language study. An even greater barrier to sharing the Gospel was the Buddhist religion, which had no concept of (or even words for) an eternal God or eternal life with God for human beings. Nonetheless, over a period of ten years, eighteen Burmese converts formed the nucleus of the first Christian church in Burma.

"Tropical fever" was the chief enemy, claiming the life of an infant son, Roger, in 1815 at the age of seven months (their first child had been stillborn on board ship). For months at a time, the dreaded fever also put both Ann and Adoniram to bed. Still, Adoniram struggled day after day to translate the Greek New Testament into the Burmese language, which he finally completed in July 1823, just before Ann returned from a two-year trip to America on medical leave.

By this time, several other missionary couples

had joined the mission in Rangoon, among them George Hough, a printer, who printed Adoniram's translation work, and Dr. Jonathan Price, a medical doctor, who was soon ordered to come to Ava, the royal city, to attend the king himself.

With other missionaries to nurture the little Burmese church in Rangoon, Adoniram and Ann also went north to Ava to establish a mission there, along with two Burmese foster daughters. But when the Burmese-British war broke out in 1824, all foreigners were suspected of being British spies and were thrown into the dreaded Death Prison. Eight months after Adoniram was arrested, Ann gave birth to a baby girl, Maria.

After a year and a half of prison confinement, Adoniram, a "neutral American," was finally released to help negotiate peace with the British. But the years of hardship, sickness, and struggle took its toll on Ann, who died in 1826 at the age of thirty-six while Adoniram was away. Two-year-old Maria died a few months later.

Adoniram tried to bury his grief in a frenzy of mission work, but later spent two years as a recluse in the jungle. When he finally pulled out of his depression, he married Sarah Boardman, a young missionary widow, who bore eight children (only five lived to adulthood) before she died after eleven years of marriage. On leave in America, Judson married young Emily Chubbock in 1846, and they returned to Burma where she became mother to Adoniram's children and their own infant daughter.

But Adoniram's own health was broken, and he died in 1850 at the age of sixty-one. His legacy included a translation of the whole Bible in the Burmese language, as well as an inspiration to other American young people to dedicate their lives to foreign missions.

For Further Reading

Anderson, Courtney, *To the Golden Shore : The Life of Adoniram Judson* (Grand Rapids, Mich.: Zondervan Publishing House, 1972).

Hubbard, Ethel Daniels, *Ann of Ava* (New York: Missionary Education Movement of the United States and Canada, 1913).

Judson, Edward (Adoniram's son, 1844-1914), *The Life of Adoniram Judson* (New York: Anson D. F. Randolph & Company, 1883).

Morrow, Honore McCue Willsie, *Splendor of God: the Life of Adoniram Judson* (Grand Rapids, Mich.: Baker Book House, 1982).

Waters, John, *Storming the Golden Kingdom: a Biography of Adoniram Judson* (Downers Grove, Ill.: InterVarsity Press, 1989).

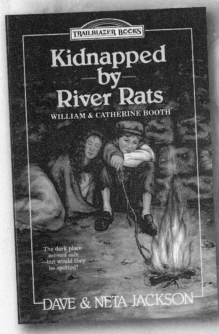

Kidnapped by River Rats

Jack and Amy have come to London searching for their uncle. On their own without money, food, or shelter, they have nowhere else to turn.

But what if they can't find him? They don't even know where he lives!

But life on the streets is filled with terrible dangers: wild dogs, thieves, rats, and kidnappers. Where can they find safety?

When those strange Salvation Army people approach them on the street, should Jack and Amy run away? Can the General and Catherine Booth be trusted?

Will they help Jack and Amy when ruthless men come after them?

For a complete listing of TRAILBLAZER BOOKS, see page 2!

"I love the TRAILBLAZER BOOKS. I can't wait to read them all!"

— Josiah, ND

Have *you* read them all? Here is a sneak peek at another TRAILBLAZER BOOK you don't want to miss!

The Bandit of Ashley Downs

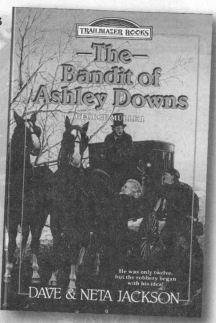

Twelve-year-old Curly is an orphan, acrobat, and master pickpocket. When he overhears that a church is raising money for an orphan house, he plans an armed robbery that promises to bring him enough money for a lifetime.

But is Curly in for more trouble than he bargained for? If he is caught, which fate would be scarier—to be sent to prison, or to the very orphanage from which he stole the money? Would George Müller, the man in charge of the orphanage, make Curly into a slave to earn back at least a portion of the money? Or might they do something even worse?

Curly is in for the biggest surprise of his young life!

For a complete listing of TRAILBLAZER BOOKS, see page 2!

✦ ✦

Series for Middle Graders* From BHP

THE ACCIDENTAL DETECTIVES • by Sigmund Brouwer
Action-packed adventures lead Ricky Kidd and his friends into places they never dreamed of, drawing them closer with every step.

ADVENTURES DOWN UNDER • by Robert Elmer
When Patrick McWaid's father is unjustly sent to Australia as a prisoner in 1867, the rest of the family follows, uncovering action-packed mystery along the way.

ADVENTURES OF THE NORTHWOODS • by Lois Walfrid Johnson
Kate O'Connell and her stepbrother Anders encounter mystery and adventure in northwest Wisconsin near the turn of the century.

BLOODHOUNDS, INC. • by Bill Myers
Hilarious, hair-raising suspense follows brother-and-sister detectives Sean and Melissa Hunter in these madcap mysteries with a message.

GIRLS ONLY! • by Beverly Lewis
Four talented young athletes become fast friends as together they pursue their Olympic dreams.

MANDIE BOOKS • by Lois Gladys Leppard
With over five million sold, the turn-of-the-century adventures of Mandie and her many friends will keep readers eager for more.

PROMISE OF ZION • by Robert Elmer
Following WWII, thirteen-year-old Dov Zalinsky leaves for Palestine—the one place he may still find his parents—and meets the adventurous Emily Parkinson. Together they experience the dangers of life in the Holy Land.

THE RIVERBOAT ADVENTURES • by Lois Walfrid Johnson
Libby Norstad and her friend Caleb face the challenges and risks of working with the Underground Railroad during the mid–1800s.

TRAILBLAZER BOOKS • by Dave and Neta Jackson
Follow the exciting lives of real-life Christian heroes through the eyes of child characters as they share their faith with others around the world.

THE YOUNG UNDERGROUND • by Robert Elmer
Peter and Elise Andersen's plots to protect their friends and themselves from Nazi soldiers in World War II Denmark guarantee fast-paced action and suspenseful reads.

*(ages 8–13)